THE STORM FROM HELL

THE STORM FROM HELL

ENOCK LYNN NORRBOM

iUniverse, Inc.
Bloomington

THE STORM FROM HELL

iUniverse books may be ordered through booksellers or by contacting:

iUniverse
1663 Liberty Drive
Bloomington, IN 47403
www.iuniverse.com
1-800-Authors (1-800-288-4677)

ISBN: 978-1-4620-5257-8 (sc)
ISBN: 978-1-4620-5258-5 (hc)
ISBN: 978-1-4620-5259-2 (ebk)

Library of Congress Control Number: 2011915943

Printed in the United States of America

iUniverse rev. date: 10/18/2011

ACKNOWLEDGMENTS

No book was ever written without the help and cooperation of many people. If I were to acknowledge all of the people who have been instrumental in writing this book, it would take another book this size.

So I will just say thank you to all of the people who have passed through my life at one time or another and contributed in ways large and small to this fantasy of reality. I would, however, like to thank my wonderful wife, Patty, for her tireless efforts and understanding during the difficult times in creating this fantasy. I would also like to thank Patty's twin sister, Peggy Mutsch, for all of her help in editing this book.

CHAPTER 1

On a hot September evening in Santa Monica, California, Jerry decided to buy a six-pack of beer to drown his sorrows. His life had been going downhill for years, first with the loss of his children to his wife in the divorce a few years before and now the loss of his last job the previous week! This might have been just about enough for Jerry. On top of all of this, Jerry's boss had told him he had a drinking problem and he should get some help.

Yes, Jerry thought to himself. *A six—pack is what this old boy needs.* A six-pack would numb the destructive thoughts he'd been having lately.

He drove up to the liquor store and got out of his truck. As he entered the liquor store, Jerry questioned what was happening to his life. He walked around the store aimlessly, feeling his life was out of control.

Jerry thought, *A six-pack ought to set me straight.* But then again, it was this very thing that had ruined his life. The drinking had left his mind in a fog and thoughts of unconcern. Jerry had scattered thoughts of his ex-wife, Sandy, with his children and the loss of his job.

Jerry's thoughts were jumbled.

Jerry Turner was a man in his early forties with a slender built, and he was considered by many to be quite good-looking. Time had added a few gray hairs around his temple, but this was very becoming on him. Twenty years ago, he seemed to have it all together—a good job as a weather forecaster, a loving wife, and two great kids. *That was a long time ago. Life is so different now,* he reflected to himself.

Jerry paid for his beer and was just leaving the liquor store. He wondered where he would go from there. He got into his pickup truck and put the six-pack in his ice chest to keep it cold. He started the truck and headed for the 405 Freeway. Jerry decided that Seal Beach was the place he would go because it was the one place that made him feel comfortable. Seal Beach usually brought back fond memories. Maybe there he could shake all these painful feelings of loneliness and despair that had been brought to life by pushing loved ones away.

Jerry had been plagued with thoughts of suicide for most of the afternoon. He thought that his life was at an end because his drinking had destroyed everything he held dear. He thought of the late nights at the bars and all the nights at home in front of the TV watching the late show and getting drunk.

"Somehow I have to shake this stinking thinking," he whispered to himself. Jerry opened the ice chest, grabbed a beer, and popped open the tab as he drove up the freeway onramp. "Drinking and driving—I'm such an inspiration!" he muttered.

Jerry really didn't need a beer. He had been drinking since he woke up that morning. Lately, drinking seemed to be his only response to his life. He would drink until he could doze off into oblivion and pass out for hours, only to awaken and start all over again. For the past week, Jerry had not slept for more than a few hours at a time after losing his last job the week before. His boss told him to go and get some help and straighten out his life. Jerry's boss really liked him and really did not want to lose him.

On the drive from Santa Monica to Seal Beach, Jerry's thoughts drifted twenty years into the past. Life was simpler then.

Jerry thought to himself, *It was my twenty forth birthday, and I was still in college studying to be a weather forecaster. My wife, Sandy, threw me a surprise birthday party. Everybody was there: my aunts, uncles, Mom, and Dad. I felt so important and loved when I walked through those big wooden doors leading into the family room. My life was on the way up, I thought. Then, I was married and twenty-four years old and finishing my master's degree. My wife and I had two children and were working on a third. My life was very good twenty years ago when I was going to school and working part time for a local weather station in Santa Monica.*

Jerry's ex-wife, Sandy, and Jerry were doing okay for themselves and were buying their first house. If only Jerry could have seen twenty years ago the destructive power that his drinking caused, he could have done something about it. That's when all the pressures of life set in. He was so overwhelmed with it all—the money, the bills, and the kids. That is when his drinking began to become a problem. He would have drinks with the boys after work and then come home and continue before and after dinner and then late into the night. It was taking its toll on his marriage. Sandy and Jerry started fighting all the time. The fights were very destructive, with words hurled about that were hard to take back once they'd been spoken.

As Jerry drove down the freeway, he thought of all the bad times that he had gone through in the past twenty years and what a waste his life had been up to this point and how his drinking and the fighting with his ex-wife had probably driven her away. At this point, Jerry's thoughts turned to his children and all of the fun that they'd had in the past twenty years—the parks, the ball games, the vacations, Disneyland, all of the time they spent fishing and playing together as a family.

Jerry thought, *Was it really worth it?"* He supposed that he was just feeling sorry for himself. Impulsively, Jerry shouted at the top of his lungs, "Life sucks!"

In the past twenty years, life had been a roller coaster. He had lost five jobs because of his drinking. His wife had left him two years ago, and his children hardly knew him anymore. His children thought he had a job on the road and only had time to see them once in a while. Jerry went to work for the past two years and either stayed at home and drank or went to the bar. Jerry did not have time to do anything but drink and feel sorry for himself. He did not even have time to see his own children, so he stayed in hiding. He reflected on his marriage and how it had ended. He had come home in the middle of the day about four years ago and found Sandy in bed with an old school friend of hers. From that time forward, his drinking got worse, until the drinking was named as one of the causes of their divorce two years later.

I knew that was not the whole truth, but it was all right with me. Jerry tried to rationalize his behavior. He did not want to believe that the divorce could also be his fault. He believed that his marriage vows were broken and there was no bona fide marriage anymore. It did not matter to him what reason his wife gave to save face. Jerry knew, and that was enough.

Jerry still loved Sandy, but to give her the rest of his life when he knew how she really felt—that was enough for him. He just got worse and worse until she could use it against him in the divorce. He felt that way because of how little the sanctity of the marriage had meant to her.

These were just some of the thoughts going through the mind of a troubled man on his way to his own suicide!

Jerry did not realize that he had driven himself into a deep depression that could very well end in disaster.

Jerry turned off the 405 Freeway on the Seventh Street off-ramp to Seal Beach. At that moment, he was unaware of some of the world events that had occurred in the past twenty-four hours. Feeling no pain, Jerry opened another can of beer and turned on the radio. While guzzling down his beer, he heard some shocking news.

"It has just been confirmed that there are at least two hurricanes in the North Pacific about 1500 miles west of North America." After hearing that statement, Jerry felt that he should be the one reporting this on the TV news broadcast right now. As Jerry pulled into the parking lot, he mumbled, as he spent his last three dollars for the parking charge.

Jerry got out of his truck, grabbed a beach towel and his ice chest full of beer, and began walking toward the beach. It was just before eight, and the sun was about to be swallowed by the Pacific in a spectacular sunset.

Jerry placed his towel near the water's edge and opened another beer. The beach looked almost empty. An old couple and three surfers walking in the direction of the pier with their surfboards under their arms were all Jerry could see. As he sat and looked out at the sunset, he could see that the tide was extremely low this evening and that it would be a full moon tonight. Jerry started to think about how his life should have turned out.

I should be the number one weather forecaster. I should have a great big house and an expensive car.

He considered his years in school when his dreams were full and life had just begun. He had the world by the tail; he was going to do such great things. He dreamed of being the number one weather forecaster in the United States.

As the sun slid past the horizon and his beer almost gone, reality hit him. More important than anything else were his children. Jerry realized how much he had destroyed his own life and grabbed another beer and chugged it down.

Jerry, now in a drunken haze, started to doze off and forgot all his troubles. As he slowly drifted away, he remembered all the fun times he had as a child.

His dad had a boat and loved to fish. Sometimes Jerry's dad would wake him up on a Saturday morning at 3:00 a.m. and tell him they were going fishing. Then he would get out of bed, grab something to eat, go help his dad get the boat ready, and hook it up to the car. His dad knew not to wake him up early on a Sunday morning, though. That was the Sabbath Day, and Grandma always took Jeremy and his family to church. And you couldn't argue with Grandma. Jerry loved the time that he spent fishing with his dad. They always had a lot of fun.

He had seen a lot of California with his dad. He had seen lakes, rivers, streams, the ocean, and many different places, like Catalina Island and San Clemente Island. Jerry always enjoyed seeing the mainland from a viewpoint out in the ocean. At night, the lights from the coastline would dance across the water like a hundred sparklers on the Fourth of July. One day in particular when they had been off the coast of Catalina Island, they had caught so many fish that the fish practically filled the inside of the boat. They were walking on and around fish everywhere in the boat. Jerry thought, *I cannot remember any other time when we caught more fish than on that trip.* Jerry and his dad had spent so much time in and around the water. Water just seemed to be a part of his life.

It's funny . . . when Jerry learned how to swim, he was at the Biltmore Hotel in Hermosa Beach, California. He was eleven or twelve years old, and everyone his age already knew how to swim. He didn't know how to swim a stroke. He dove into the deep end of the pool where all his friends were and came up at the edge of the pool. The fourth time, Jerry didn't make it to the edge and a lifeguard had to save him. He told Jerry to go to the shallow end and not to come back to the deep end until he learned to swim. It scared Jerry so much that he had almost drowned before the lifeguard got to him, and he was determined that that would never happen to him again. He really wanted to be at the deep end with his friends, so he learned to swim that very day. It is funny what you can do when you really have a need.

Jerry got up and tried to compose his thoughts. It was about 10:00 p.m. Finishing his last beer, Jerry got off the towel he'd been laying on and began walking toward the water. Suddenly, he noticed that something was wrong. He couldn't hear the surf, and when he squinted to take a better look, he couldn't see any water. The night lights were on at the beach but were not bright enough. Where there should have been water, there wasn't any! Jerry began walking out toward the ocean, feeling panicky and very confused.

Jerry began walking out even farther and still could not see any water. The only thing that lit his path was the moon. Then he began to run. He ran faster and faster, his heart beating rapidly, when he suddenly fell into a big pool of water. He fell into the water headfirst and got soaking wet. When he rolled over, he found himself sitting in a pool of water about half the size of a football field and about two feet deep.

Well at least I found some water, he thought.

But then the realization of just where he was hit him as a fish brushed by his arm and another by his back. Startled, Jerry jumped to his feet just in time to see a sand shark slither into deeper water. He could see that he was at the edge of a large pool of water where great numbers of fish had been caught by the receding waters. But this was not the only water that Jerry could see in the dim light. Looking, around he could see other pools nearby, but he still could not hear the surf.

Jerry really began to worry now, and he stopped to collect his thoughts. He was in the pool of water with thousands of fish churning where they were trapped.

You could walk on all of those fish, Jerry thought.

Jerry began to rise out of the water. He then walked around the pool and looked harder, as the moonlight made it a bit easier to see. He started to investigate this strange and eerie sight that reminded him of photos he had seen of the tides receding in other countries.

Jerry walked for what seemed to be a lifetime, looking and trying to figure out just what was going on. Then, out of the corner of his eye, he spotted something in the distance. As he turned to get a better look, he could see one individual. Then, as he drew closer, he could see more than one person. As Jerry looked around, he noticed that he was not the only person who had discovered that the tide had withdrawn, as there were hundreds of people out looking to find out what had happened.

Just then Jerry heard someone say, "Hey! Do you know what is going on here?"

"I don't have a clue. Do you?" replied Jerry.

"No," the stranger said, "but it is all over the news."

"What is all over the news?" Jerry asked.

The stranger replied, "Didn't you hear on the news that the water has receded all up and down the coast and in some places it is gone for twenty miles? Boats are lying on their sides in some harbors. Others are stuck at sea and can't get to shore because the water is too shallow."

All the people at the beach with Jerry were in a frenzied panic, and no one knew what was going on. Someone said there was a tidal wave coming and that was why the water was receding, but no one knew for sure just what was happening. Everyone was talking and giving his or her opinion.

Jerry now noticed countless people at the beach. The moon was three-quarters full, and even though it was about 11:00 at night, Jerry was able to see a lot better now. Jerry could see fisherman from the pier with gunnysacks. They were filling the sacks with fish as fast as they could.

One fisherman had about six or seven bags full beside the pool he was working in. Everywhere he looked, Jerry could see people carrying fish to the dry sand.

Jerry suddenly heard a loud flapping sound and turned his head in the direction of the sound. Just then it caught his eye—a shark about six feet long stranded between two small pools. As he turned to walk toward the shark, he stepped on something slimy and almost fell on his face. As he looked down to see just what it was, he looked straight at a spiny rockfish, and he felt glad he had shoes on. He got to the shark and found it was a blue shark. It was a female, and she was giving birth to about a dozen baby sharks. Jerry had seen this many times before. When you catch a female shark that has babies and she knows she's going to die, she gives birth, hoping that some will survive. She did not have much fight left in her. Jerry knew it was over for that blue shark. Somehow it grieved him.

Just then Jerry heard a loud scream and looked up to see a young girl about sixteen years old splashing in a pool about twenty yards away. He ran to see what he could do to help her. Once Jerry got to the girl, he helped her out of the pool and saw she had no shoes on and had probably stepped on a stingray. Her foot was swollen and bleeding. Jerry looked up to see if he could find someone to help. In the distance, he could see lights from a vehicle and could tell that it was a lifeguard, so he called for help. He waved his arms frantically to get the lifeguard's attention.

"Hey, man," shouted Jerry. "This girl's really been hurt. I need your help."

The lifeguard stopped to see what was going on and helped the girl into his jeep.

"I don't understand all of this," said the lifeguard, "but I've been getting a lot of calls down by the pier. I have to go. I'll take care of the girl. She'll be fine." He quickly sped off.

With all the commotion going on, it took a while to realize a few hours had already passed. Jerry noticed that he was not in a mental fog any longer. In fact, it was like he had not taken a drink at all. The reality of all of this had sobered him up.

There seemed to be a lot of noise coming from about two hundred yards away by some rocks. Jerry started to move in the direction of the rocks. There were a lot of lights and people around the edge of the rocks, and as Jerry got closer, he still could not see everything, but he could hear some whistling or high-pitched screaming. Jerry didn't understand until he got much closer and could see three or four dolphins caught in a small pool of water—too small, in fact, for them to survive, and the people around were talking and pointing their flashlights at them. Once Jerry reached them, he asked, "Does anyone know just what has caused the water to recede?"

Just then an older man answered, "Well I don't know for sure, but the news says that the entire west coast is just like this and no one seems to know why."

By this time, Jerry had heard and seen enough to understand that he needed access to more information before he could put this whole puzzle right in his mind. He had some ideas that he had formed in his mind, but they were too scary to think about at this point. Jerry turned and began to walk toward the dry sand and the parking lot. As he walked, the thoughts that were going through his mind were too horrifying to cope with.

Jerry thought to himself, *If this is what it looks and sounds like, this could be the beginning of the end. This could be the Colossus Tri-Hurricane Tornado Phenomena that I wrote my mid-term paper on in college, and that is too horrifying to think about!*

He started to feel frightened and began walking faster and faster until the walking became running.

As Jerry got to the dry sand, his running got harder and harder until his feet started dragging, and then he fell. He got up in a panic and ran as quickly as he could. He stumbled three or four more times before he got to the asphalt parking lot. Jerry was so tired and out of breath that he collapsed to his knees and sat there for a few minutes to catch his breath and try and regain his composure. That's when his mind made a leap toward his children and to what he could do to help them. Jerry got up, exhausted and weak, but managed to walk to the payphone. Depositing coins in the phone, he called his former wife, Sandy.

The phone rang for what seemed to be a lifetime before Sandy answered the phone.

"Sandy, this is Jerry. I'm at the beach. Have you heard the news about the receding waters?"

"Well," she replied hesitantly, "yes. Is it true that the water has receded by as much as twenty miles?"

"Yes it's true," said Jerry. "I just ran to the phone from where the water used to be."

"What do you mean by that remark?" cried Sandy.

"I'm not sure," said Jerry, "but I'm going to get more information when I get off the phone with you, and I should know more by morning. It doesn't look good. It could only be half a dozen different things, and half of those could be devastating. So I am asking you to get in touch with the kids and take the kids and their families to your aunt's house in Montana tomorrow.

"I have a bank account at the First State Bank down the street from your house, and there is $14,000 in the account. Take it and the kids get on a plane, and I will call you at your aunt's house as soon as I can."

"What are you talking about, Jerry?" Sandy shouted. "This is crazy!"

"Please, let's not bicker with one another," Jerry said. "If everything turns out to be okay, it will be like a mini-vacation for you and the children."

Sandy replied, "The bank will not let me take money out of your account."

Jerry asked, "Sandy do you have our old bank account number?"

"No," Sandy said.

Jerry pulled out his card. "Here are the numbers, Sandy—468, 258, 8890, and the expiration is 8/12." Sandy wrote the numbers as Jerry read them off.

"I will stop at the ATM and transfer the money to that account. Then you can take it from that account, okay?"

"Okay, but this sounds crazy!" Sandy replied.

They said their good-byes, and Jerry hung up the phone. He turned to look for his truck. It seemed to be a hundred miles away as he started walking. When he got to the truck, he put the key in the door and unlocked it, got in, and as he closed the door, the exhaustion from the run up the beach to the parking lot finally hit him. Jerry sat there in his truck for about ten minutes trying to decide what his next move would be.

Suddenly, like a flash of lightning, it hit him. "Tom! Yes! That's the answer. I will go and see Tom. He will be absorbed in the computer by now attempting to find out what is going on."

Jerry started his truck and headed for Tom's place. He saw a lot of emergency vehicles on their way to the beach with sirens blazing—police cars, fire trucks, paramedics, and ambulances. The city seemed to be alive with disaster this very night.

Jerry spotted a bank and pulled his truck into the parking lot, parked next to the ATM, and transferred the money from his account to their old joint account. Jerry also got one hundred dollars for himself, not knowing just what would happen next. Having finished with the bank, Jerry left the parking lot and headed for Tom's place.

While going over a bridge, Jerry could see a half a dozen boats on their sides. *They sure look funny that way*, Jerry thought.

Jerry thoughts flashed back to a time when he was on a three-day fishing trip at Catalina Island. His dad and he had spent the night at Catalina harbor on the far side of the island. During the night, the tide had gone out and left some boats on their sides. It was a funny sight then, but it didn't seem so funny now.

Looking back toward the bridge, Jerry could see one boat hanging from the dock. One end of a rope was tied to the cleats of the boat, and the other end was tied to the cleats on the dock. There was two feet of empty space between the boat and the sand. Jerry knew it wouldn't be long before either the ropes or the cleats give out and the boat would fall to the sand.

It took hours to drive to Tom's place, even though it was just a few miles away. The traffic was hideous. There were thousands of people heading for the beach by car and on foot.

Jerry guessed that everyone just wanted to see what the news media had been talking about for the past few hours.

"Boy, it's been a long night!" he said aloud to himself.

CHAPTER 2

Jerry continued to drive up Ocean Boulevard toward Long Beach to see his friend Tom. Tom had a degree in computer science. Tom believed in Jerry, and he shared the same passion for the weather. Tom and Jerry had been friends since they first met in high school. From that first day in gym, all they talked about was weather and computers. Neither of them liked sports. They spent their time learning from one another, and that brought them closer together. They were bonded tight. Jerry had spent a lot of time with Tom through the years riding in Tom's plane looking at weather patterns. He co-piloted with Tom on many flights. Tom was also a computer hacker, and using the computer for weather variations brought wide and vast knowledge to him. He was always on his computer working out immeasurable data that somehow could help Jerry see the weather patterns from a wider prospective. It made Jerry follow these patterns more closely.

Traffic was very congested, and Jerry had already been driving for several hours. He was relieved he didn't have much farther to go to get to Tom's.

I can't wait to get to Tom's, thought Jerry. *Tom will understand why I'm so tense.*

Jerry finally pulled into the parking lot where Tom's office was located. He was so happy to have finally arrived that he felt a sort of nervous excitement hit him as he turned into the driveway to park the truck. Not paying attention to what was going on at this time, he ran right into a new Caddy as he was driving at about twenty miles an hour. The accident did a lot of damage to the Cadillac's right front fender and to his own left front fender. Immediately after the collision, a stunning woman got out of the smashed car roaring like a tiger and pointing her finger in his face.

"What kind of jerk are you? Didn't anyone ever show you how to drive?" the woman said.

Jerry said, "You're right and I am very sorry, but we can't do anything here. Why don't we park our cars and go inside the Jolly Roger restaurant just ahead and have a cup of coffee? Then we can exchange license and insurance information."

The woman began to quarrel with him about this so-called token action of his, but Jerry did not budge. Hesitantly, she agreed because she found him quite attractive.

"Well, I suppose it wouldn't hurt anything. After all, I need your insurance information," she said.

Jerry turned and walked back to his truck, got in, and turned the ignition key. As he maneuvered the truck into a parking place, he said to the woman, "I will park your car next if you like."

"Okay." She sighed.

Jerry got out of his truck and went to the front of the Caddy to see if there would be any tire damage if he moved the car.

"Your tire will be okay when I move the car," Jerry said as he reached for the keys from the woman. Jerry parked the Caddy and locked it. Then he turned to the woman and dropped the keys into her hand.

They proceeded into the coffee shop, and Jerry observed how striking this woman was. She wore a dark blue skirt and an ocean blue silk blouse that matched the color of her eyes. She had soft black hair and a flawless complexion, and her blue eyes were almond shaped. Her thin features were further defined by a delicately shaped nose and arched eyebrows. Her soft lips were highlighted with a very soft rose lipstick. In short, she was beautiful. Jerry looked at her, and he was enchanted. They were greeted at the host stand, and Jerry said, "Two please!" The host quickly seated them.

"My name is Lydia Walsh," she grunted, "and haven't I seen you somewhere before?"

Jerry sensed a spark of fire coming from this striking woman—a fire he'd like to put out.

"My name is Jerry Turner, and I think I would remember if we had met before."

The waitress came to the table, and Jerry ordered coffee for them both. They began to exchange insurance information. Then Jerry asked the waitress about the news.

"Did you hear anything about the ocean water?"

Immediately another waitress spoke up and said, "It is on the news right now," pointing to the TV on the wall.

Jerry asked, "Could you turn up the volume?"

The waitress walked over to the TV and turned up the volume. The TV media was vague; at best, they didn't seem to know much about the storms.

"You're Jerry Turner," Lydia said. "You're the same Jerry Turner who is on the TV news!"

Jerry said, "Yes, I am that newsman. Why? Did you watch me on the news?"

Jerry's ego started inflating.

"I knew you looked familiar," she said. "I watched you for years until I moved to the Cape in Florida with my dad. He works down there for NASA Weather. You know, we used to talk about you. Dad says you know a lot about the weather and that you're not just one of those know-it-all college boys. He said that you really understand the weather and have a love for it."

Jerry said, "Thank you. That means a lot to me."

Jerry thought to himself, *How could I be so fortunate to have this gorgeous woman watching me on TV?*

Suddenly, Jerry remembered what he had come there to do. He blurted out, "Oh my God, I forgot! I'm supposed to be next door. I was coming down here to see a friend of mine. He knows much more than this TV station does about these storms. He is hooked into satellite tracking. Lydia, would you like to go with me and see if we can find out just what is going on? We can finish giving each other our insurance information over at his place. It's just next door."

Lydia hesitated, and somehow, against her better judgment she agreed. She didn't know why, but she felt compelled to go with this stranger. Jerry paid for the coffee, and they walked next door to see Tom.

Jerry rang the bell two or three times before Tom came to the door.

Tom opened the door, and he said sharply, "Come in and meet me in the office. I am hooked up to the satellite tracking."

Tom rushed back to his office. Jerry and Lydia came in and shut the door. Jerry showed Lydia to the office where Tom was watching a satellite broadcast from NASA Weather. Larry Walsh, the head at NASA Weather, was speaking about the storms in the North Pacific Ocean.

"The last satellite pictures showed some very disturbing storms, and it could be morning before we have a better understanding of what is going on."

"Hey, that's my dad," said Lydia.

Tom said, "You've got to be kidding!"

Lydia replied, "I will show you."

She opened her purse and took out a small photo album that had photos of her father and herself. As they looked at the photos, they found their eyes turning toward the TV. Lydia's father continued talking about the storm.

"These are satellite photos taken yesterday, and it clearly shows three hurricanes in a triangle about six hundred miles apart. Today you cannot see the hurricanes because there seems to be a tornado sitting in the middle of the hurricanes. This is very confusing, because these are two different kinds of storms. We hope to have more information tomorrow from the satellites. At this time, we are sending some US coast guard Weather planes into the storm. This is Larry Walsh from NASA Weather, and I will report any new information as it comes in."

"Wow! I wish that I could be there, because this sounds like a dream come true," Jerry said.

Tom and Lydia turned to look at him like he was out of his mind.

"Jerry," Tom said, "are you out of your mind?"

"No," Jerry insisted. "I majored in weather, and all I could think of was weather and weather patterns, hurricanes, tornadoes, and storms, as you well know, Tom. But this is a chance of a lifetime. You know that these storms and the way that they are acting look just like what I wrote my midterm papers on. Colossus Tri-Hurricane Tornado Phenomena! That is a theory that Einstein had that no one has ever been able to prove."

"Jerry," Lydia said, "I heard my dad say something about that, but I can't remember just what it was."

"Okay," Jerry said. "Einstein had this theory that if three hurricanes start close enough to each other and you add cold air or water in a summer condition to react to each other, you know, like an air-conditioning unit, they could cause a tornado to start in the center of the hurricanes. That could be more devastating than anything man has ever seen on this earth before. His theory uses these three hurricanes as motors to power or run the tornado. So in theory, when you take these three hurricanes that are surrounding a tornado and add ice water, with a mass of air moving at a high rate of speed, it could act just like a refrigerator to form ice. The ice could form a wall around the outside of the tornado to create a vacuum pump that would suck up the water into the center of the tornado."

Tom looked at Jerry and said, "Are you thinking what I am thinking?"

"Yes," replied Jerry. "Let's see this thing for ourselves! All the pieces are there. If this is what I think it is, we have to know! We just have to!"

Lydia blurted out, "I'm going too!"

"No, it is too dangerous," replied Jerry.

Tom agreed.

"Hey, guys, wait just a minute here. If this storm is as unique as I think it is, I need to see it for myself. Besides, you may need my help convincing people of your theories. I majored in public relations, and I know everyone in the weather world. You have to have someone they will listen to. And I'm sure I can convince my dad. I am the girl for you." Lydia was confident.

"*I am going,* and that is that!" she replied.

Jerry smiled at Lydia. He thought, *Well, she is quite the stubborn one. When she talks she has such conviction in her voice that everyone has to listen.*

"If it is okay with Tom, then it is okay with me," Jerry said with a smile on his face.

Tom said, "Okay. There are a lot of things that we have to do in order to make this happen. First of all, this is going to be a fifteen—to twenty-hour trip. Is anyone hungry?"

"Well, kind of," said Jerry.

"I could go for something," said Lydia.

"Does anyone want to help throw something together?" Tom asked.

Lydia answered, "I can. I happen to be a very good cook. Just wait until you've tasted my cooking! Just show me the kitchen and where everything is. I'll take care of everything else."

"Well we need to pack a lunch besides eating something now. Thanks so much, Lydia. I hope I am not asking too much," said Tom.

Tom took Lydia to the kitchen and showed her where everything was—the food, seasonings, pots and pans, cooking utensils, and anything else she would need.

As he turned to go back to the office, he said, "You have about an hour before we have to leave. Oh, and by the way, I am Tom, and I am so glad to meet you, Lydia."

Tom walked into the office and saw Jerry working frantically on the computer. "Jerry, you know this is going to be a very dangerous trip."

Jerry answered, "Are you kidding? This is the chance of a lifetime!"

"Always the stubborn one, aren't you? Jerry, we have a lot of packing to do, and we need lots of supplies. We need to get it done. There is not much time," Tom said.

They all worked feverishly. Within forty-five minutes, Lydia had breakfast on the table and was calling Tom and Jerry to come to eat. Lydia sat down at the table and began to serve herself. Tom and Jerry were not quite done with the things they had to do, but they were hungry, so they left their first priority for a little while and came to the table.

When Tom and Jerry entered the kitchen, they could not believe their eyes. The aroma was like being at a country feast. The table was laden like it was a piece of art. There were fried potatoes with grilled onions, smoked bacon, fluffy pancakes, biscuits and creamed gravy, fresh-squeezed orange juice, and scrambled eggs. There were also breakfast rolls and sausages. The smell of freshly brewed coffee filled the air.

Tom said cheerfully, "This is better than going to a restaurant! I have never seen so much food on this table."

As Jerry started eating, he thought, *Where has this woman been all of my life? Any man lucky enough to find himself married to this remarkable woman would be the luckiest man alive.* Jerry was moving too fast in his mind, and he knew it.

While stuffing his face, Tom spoke out, "Where did you learn to cook like this, Lydia?"

"My dad." Lydia smirked.

"What other surprises do you have in store for us in your bag of tricks? You know, if I ate like this every day, I would be as big as a house. We wouldn't be able to take off because the plane would be too overloaded." Tom chuckled.

They all started laughing.

Tom looked up at Lydia and said, "If you can cook like this, how come you're not married? Any man would like to eat like this and have a beautiful woman like you on his arm any time of the day or night."

Lydia's face got flushed.

"I haven't found a man that can take care of business and have the compassion that it takes to handle a woman like me."

Tom had noticed that Lydia had no ring on her left ring finger within the first five minutes of meeting her. He also knew it was Jerry who really intrigued her.

Tom's conversation changed abruptly to the trip they were about to embark on. "Okay, we need to bring a new program that I have just worked out last week. This program will help us to calculate airspeed and water speed with the computer. Jerry, do not let me forget this program when we leave."

Lydia spoke out, "Can you really determine the speed with a computer?"

"Yes!" Tom proudly said. "With this program, I can do just that! You see, I send a sound blast into the water, and it bounces three times, and it comes back. The time between the bounces gives the computer a measurement, and it will tell me how fast the water is moving. Air was a little harder to figure out. I finally found that I could use a solid screech and the air would turn it into a wave like a solid line. Now I calculate the distance between the waves, minus the frequency of the screeches, plus the radius of the wave and there you have it! The speed of the air! This one was really hard to figure out. I have been working on this for three or four years and have just finished it in the last few weeks."

They finished breakfast and immediately got to work again cleaning up the dishes and packing the lunch Lydia made for the trip. Tom went to the office for a last-minute check on the satellite position of the storm.

Jerry came in and said, "How is it going? By the way, don't forget the program!"

Tom said, "I got it!"

Lydia came in and said, "Don't forget the speed program."

"I got it. Man you guys are a pain," Tom said, chuckling.

"Tom, where's the porta-potty?" Jerry asked.

"In the bedroom at the bottom of the closet, and the chemicals are in a blue and white box on the shelf next to the shoebox," Tom said.

"That is why we were late for breakfast. We were figuring just how to make a bathroom in the plane with a curtain for privacy so you won't feel embarrassed when you have to use the potty." Jerry grinned.

"You guys thought about everything," said Lydia sheepishly. "You know, I am so excited I can hardly believe that we are really going."

Jerry said, "I know just what you mean. I have butterflies in my stomach."

"Yes, I feel the same way too. No one has ever seen what we are about to see. Ever!" said Tom.

"Yes, just think, three hurricanes in the same area," Lydia said.

They all got into Tom's car and drove to the airport, which was only three blocks away. When they arrived, they got out of the car, grabbed their things from the trunk, and proceeded toward the hanger. Lydia's mouth dropped open. There it was—a 1967 Grumman HU-16E Albatross with two like-new 1,425-hp Cyclone radial piston engines. Tom had rebuilt the engines himself and boosted the power two times the original power.

"Each engine produces over 2,500 hp, and this Seaplane that the builder said could only fly at 250 mph can now fly at 500 mph. And the plane is not very big," said Tom. "She is only sixty-one feet in length with a wingspan of ninety-six feet, but oh this baby can fly." Tom talked about his Albatross as if it were his only love.

When Lydia looked at the plane, she expected to see a new Coast guard seaplane that had all the bells and whistles. Instead what she saw was a World War two seaplane that looked like it belonged in a museum.

Before she could stop herself, she said, "You are kidding me, aren't you?"

A look came over Tom's face that told Lydia she had made a mistake saying what she said.

To cover her backside, she said, "Tom, if you are as good of a mechanic as you are on a computer, then this plane is as good as, if not better than a new one?" This seemed to suffice for the time.

Tom looked at Lydia with a smile on his face and said, "We will not have any problems. This plane is just as good as brand new. Just wait until we get in the air. You will see she runs like a new Caddy, and she is as strong as a bull."

Caddy, Lydia thought to herself. It was the accident that had brought her to this place with these two men. *Life has its purposes,* she quietly thought to herself

Jerry had a look on his face like a lightning bolt had just hit him between the eyes. Then he began to speak to Tom with a broken voice. "Tom, I just remembered there is no water! How in the world are we going to take off?"

"You know, this plane does have wheels. But we do have a problem because this runway is too short for all the weight we are carrying. I think we're over weight. I am not sure by how much, but I think it is quite a bit."

CHAPTER 3

Because there wasn't any water for miles, they had to use the runway at this little airport to take off. The runway was so short they couldn't take off. Jerry then spotted a forklift and noticed that the parking lot at the end of the runway was empty. The only thing separating the two was a chain link fence. Jerry said to Tom, "If I cut that fence down at the end of the runway, do you think that will give us enough room to take off?"

"It looks like we just might make it," Tom said.

Jerry grabbed a cutting torch and the gas bottles from the hanger as he ran to the forklift. He jumped on the forklift and headed for the fence. When Jerry got to the fence, he went to one end and quickly cut one end of the fence off the pole. Then he hooked the cut end of the fence to the forks of the forklift and jumped back on it and literally tore down the fence far enough for the plane to fit through. He then cut the fence poles down at the ground with the torch and dragged the poles to the side of the runway. Jerry climbed back onto the forklift and rushed back to the plane where Tom and Lydia were waiting.

Tom said to Jerry, "I hope this will give us enough room to take off. After all, we are over weight with these fuel and oxygen tanks."

Jerry took the forklift and parked it and then ran to the plane, where Tom was waiting for him with four oxygen bottles.

"Jerry," Tom said, "help me put these new bottles in the plane."

Tom jumped in the plane. Jerry began to push the bottles up into the plane where Tom was waiting to pull them the rest of the way in. Jerry jumped into the plane to help Tom with the bottles of oxygen.

"We will put them against that wall, pointing at the far wall across from the door," Tom said.

They put the bottles of oxygen away and secured them to the plane's wall with straps. Tom got out of the plane and ran back to his car. He came back with two thermoses of coffee and a flashlight, and he jumped in and said, "All aboard!"

Lydia and Jerry were already seated and strapped in for takeoff. Jerry had put Lydia in the right seat for the takeoff and sat himself in front of the computers in the back of the plain behind Tom for the takeoff.

"Okay, hold on, we're taking off," said Tom.

Tom hit the throttles on the airplane, and they began to move. As they moved down the runway, the opening in the chain-link fence kept getting closer, but it didn't seem like they were going fast enough. They thought that they just might not make it off the ground. As they passed the hole in the chain link fence, they were praying to lift off the ground. The end of the parking lot past the runway seemed to be close enough to reach out and touch. But as they got to the end of the parking lot, the plane lifted from the ground, and they made it into the air by the skin of their teeth.

The sunlight was just breaking over the east of the mountains as they climbed a few hundred feet over Long Beach. As they turned the plane to go over the harbor and out to sea to set a course for the storm, they could hardly believe their eyes. There was not very much water in the Long Beach harbor. The most amazing sight was the marinas that held small boats.

"God, look at all those boats. There is no water for them," said Lydia.

"Almost all marinas are built with about twenty feet of water under the boats," Jerry said.

All the marinas were empty, and the boats were on dry sand. The only water to be found was where the shipping lanes were. The outer harbor had very little water. It was an amazing sight. Big ships could be seen sitting on their bottoms everywhere. What a strange sight that was. Sailboats could be seen all over the harbor lying on their sides.

"It looks like an air traffic jam up here over the harbor," Tom said.

When they looked out of the plane, they saw police, news, and coast guard helicopters all over the place. There were airplanes everywhere. It was like a traffic jam in downtown LA, except this was in the air over the Long Beach harbor.

"Look at all the people. They all look like ants!" Lydia said.

As they looked up and down the coast, they could see people everywhere by the thousands.

"Look at the breakwater wall. It looks like a giant snake," Jerry said. "I can see it all the way to San Pedro."

They circled the Long Beach Harbor two times, and at the Seal Beach end, they saw vast areas of sand, some extending out for about five to ten miles.

As they left the coastline of Long Beach, it was so startling they could hardly believe their eyes!

"Gosh, this is something like I've never seen," said Tom.

As they left the coast, there were a lot of boats a few miles from shore. It looked like a Sunday afternoon in the summer time. There were eight or ten big ships waiting twenty to forty miles offshore because there were no functional shipping lanes to bring these big ships to the harbor.

They started flying over Catalina Island. Catalina was at least one-half times bigger than it was before. Every harbor was empty of water, and half of the boats were sitting on dry sand. Most boats were on their bottoms, and of course, the sailboats were on their sides.

"I have flown over Catalina at least one hundred times, and I have never seen it look like this. It is so much bigger than before this storm thing," Tom exclaimed.

The plane began to climb to an altitude of five thousand feet.

"Set the course to one hundred and seventy degrees west to the storm. Then show Lydia how to set the autopilot and explain to Lydia to keep her eyes on the instruments," said Tom.

Tom left Lydia to join Jerry at the computer.

"Jerry, can you help me with the oxygen tanks? We need to hook the tanks to these panels that feed the engines and our oxygen masks," said Tom.

Jerry went to the back of the plane and grabbed the toolbox and brought it over to the oxygen tanks. Tom started to work frantically on the oxygen tanks by hooking all of them to a panel on the side of the plane. When Tom was finished, Tom took Jerry to the middle of the plane where the computer system was. Tom called Lydia back to the computers, where he showed her and Jerry five computer screens and began to tell them all the settings to monitor if Tom was too busy to come back and do it himself. Jerry put a set of headphones on. Tom went back to the cockpit to put on his own headphones and asked Lydia to put her headphones on also. Tom began to describe to Jerry and Lydia key information about the computers systems that they might need to monitor the storm's patterns. Then, for the next four hours, Tom coached Lydia and Jerry on how to check the weather patterns. Tom also explained to them how to use the new programs for checking the air and water speed.

Meanwhile in Alaska, a plane piloted by William P. Gunnerson of the US Coast Guard Hurricane Watch was getting ready to take off after refueling. The US Coast Guard Weather Bureau at NASA had ordered Captain Gunnerson, cheerfully known as Gunner to all of his friends and his crew, to Alaska to investigate the strange happenings in the North Pacific Ocean.

Very large icebergs were breaking off and drifting southward, which could be a danger to the shipping in the area, but the main concern was the abnormal amount of cold water that was flowing southward, as interpreted by the satellite!

After takeoff, Gunner and his crew were experiencing the same feelings that Tom, Jerry, and Lydia had experienced on the coastline of California. The receding water caused the boats to lie on their sides and on their bottoms. Gunner was an old friend of Tom's, but they hadn't seen each other in months.

When Gunner and his crew had flown out about 150 miles, an iceberg approximately sixty miles long and twenty miles wide appeared. They flew around it for about twenty minutes. They estimated that it was moving at a speed of ten miles per hour, which was incredibly fast for an iceberg. There were also unusual amounts of smaller icebergs in the area. Some were the size of houses and some the size of a small rural town. There were hundreds of these icebergs. Visibility was at least one hundred miles, as it was a bright and sunny day. But what concerned Gunner was this river of ice water that was flowing south.

Gunner turned the plane south by southwest, following the river in the direction of a coast guard cutter. It had been charting the river, checking the speed, depth, and width. It was about eighty miles from Gunner and his crew. They could barely make out the cutter in the distance. They could see the wake from the boat moving through the water, which made it look like a snake moving back and forth across the river of ice that was moving southward in the great Pacific Ocean. Following this river was not a very hard task. Sometimes it was hard to make out the river itself. But because of all the icebergs being pulled by the river, it made it easier to follow the flow of the river.

The cutter was a B class, 160 feet long and weighing two hundred tons. It had a complement of sixty-five men and could reach a speed of forty-eight knots.

Gunner had been talking with the captain on his radio. Captain Jack Housen and Gunner exchanged thoughts and small talk. Their crews were exchanging and collecting all the information their crews could collect. Gunner asked Captain Housen about the river, like the speed, the depth, and width and temperature.

Captain Housen replied to Gunner, "The ice-cold water is mostly fresh and heavier than sea water, so they do not mix together well. The sea water temperature is about fifty to sixty degrees this time of year, but the temperature of the fresh water varies a little, only about five degrees, and that is just above freezing, which is thirty-three to thirty-eight degrees, and it remains constant. I have given this information to your crew and to the Coast Guard Communication Center. I reported that the river was crawling along the bottom of the sea like a snake moving around underwater hills and mountains, through valleys and shallows. You are heading for an iceberg that seems to be the biggest that I've ever heard of and it is dead ahead.

Gunner thanked Captain Housen for all of the information and wished them a safe journey.

Gunner brought the nose of his plane down to about five hundred feet as they approached the cutter. Then Captain Housen explained to Gunner that the iceberg was ninety-five to one hundred and five miles dead ahead.

After passing the cutter, Gunner looked up from his plane to see if he could see the iceberg. What he saw was identical to looking at the coastlines. As far as he could see to the east and the west, it looked like the coastline. So Gunner pulled back on the wheel of the plane, and it lifted and leveled off at five thousand feet, continuing on toward the iceberg. After about twenty minutes, they could see that the iceberg was huge and hovering over the river like a worm underneath a house. Gunner climbed back up to thirty thousand feet so he could get a better overall look at this iceberg. After leveling off at thirty thousand feet, Gunner could see that this iceberg was probably one hundred to one hundred and twenty five miles across.

This has to be the monster of all icebergs, he thought.

So Gunner brought his plane back down to two thousand feet. What seemed to be a lifetime of mountaintop skipping and valley running through ice picks actually was only thirty-five minutes. They neared the other side of the iceberg about 105 miles across from north to south.

As they were nearing the other side of the iceberg, one of the crew members yelled out over the intercom that he could see smoke and what looked like a small Eskimo village. Gunner took the plane down to about five hundred feet to investigate. When he got low enough, he started a circling pattern. Gunner saw a small Eskimo village with about twenty homes and about forty or fifty people all waving their arms at the Coast Guard plane in anticipation of being rescued. Gunner told his radioman to see if he could get in touch with the Eskimo village.

"Gunner, this is Davis. I have the chief of the Eskimo village on the intercom. His name is Chef Mukluk, and he sounds very happy to see us."

After talking with Chef Mukluk of the Eskimo village for about ten minutes, Gunner assured them that he would contact the Coast Guard and send help immediately. Gunner took his plane out of a circling pattern and headed south, following the river again and climbing to twenty thousand feet. After contacting the Coast Guard Communication Center and explaining the situation of the Eskimo village and their exact location, Gunner was assured that a large rescue party of helicopters and Coast Guard ships were on their way. Gunner breathed a sigh of relief.

Just then, one of the crew members of Gunner's plane broke in over the intercom to tell Gunner about something strange he had seen around the river. Gunner decided to bring the plane back down to one thousand feet to investigate this further. What they found was very strange indeed. Around the sides of the river were great swirls, like whirlpools on both sides of the river. Some were larger than others. After a brief discussion with the crew, it was decided that it must be the speed of the river flowing through the ocean that caused these whirlpool-like swirls. The consensus on board the plane was that this river must be moving at a speed ranging from twenty to thirty miles per hour. Because of their experiences on rivers like the Columbia, the Snake, and the Colorado River, where there are great swirls or whirlpools, they concluded that this could only be caused by fast-moving water.

Gunner called Captain Housen on the coast guard cutter and asked him how fast the river was flowing.

Captain Housen answered, "Twenty-one knots, sir," which is just over twenty-four miles per hour.

Meanwhile, about one thousand miles away, Tom, Jerry, and Lydia were about fifty miles from the first storm and had climbed to an altitude of forty thousand feet. They were all wearing oxygen masks, and Tom had been explaining to Jerry and Lydia about all the extra oxygen bottles. He explained how he had hooked oxygen bottles to the engine carburetors so that if the engines didn't get enough air, he would use the oxygen from the tanks. Looking out the front windows, they could see the first hurricane. It looked awesome.

I've seen twenty-two of these great hurricanes, but it never changes. It always looks like death, Tom thought to himself.

Just then, Lydia mentioned to Tom, "What are all of those funny looking things in the water? They look like ice cubes."

Tom said sarcastically, "They're called icebergs, Lydia." And he rolled his eyes.

"Isn't that unusual out here at this time of year?" Lydia said.

"Yes," Tom answered. "That's unusual. So is that river that is just coming up."

"What river?" Lydia asked.

"Do you see that dark color just ahead that looks like a snake?" Tom asked.

Lydia shouted, "I see it, I see it!"

They were flying over the first hurricane now. Looking down, they could see the eye of it. But the most foreboding sight they had ever seen in all their lives appeared before them. As high as their eyes could see, a wall of water and ice stood before them.

The bottom of the wall was made of solid ice, the upper half ice and water. And then curving above them were mist and clouds so thick they couldn't see above it. The wall of the tornado was one hundred miles away from them but so magnificent that they could see it from very far away.

"Lydia," Tom said, "it is time to take the plane off autopilot and start climbing. We are at forty thousand feet." Tom began a slow climb, and for the next one hundred miles they climbed and climbed. Now at eighty thousand feet they had to run the plane on oxygen from the tanks as they approached the wall of the storm. The turbulence was so bad that they had to hold on with one hand all the time.

Tom and Jerry had been discussing that the only way they could get through the wall of this storm was to fly with the wind in a counterclockwise direction and try to break through the wall. They set their course and turned the plane counterclockwise and entered the wall in the same direction that the wall was moving. The turbulence was so bad that they had to hold on with both hands now.

The wind speed inside the wall was over two hundred miles per hour. After fifteen minutes, they found that they didn't make much progress, so they decided to put the plane into a dive to try to get more speed. Tom found that the plane was almost too hard to handle, so he told Lydia to trade places with Jerry, and it felt like playing bumper cars inside a telephone booth. By the time Jerry got in the right seat and got buckled in, Tom really needed his help. The plane was almost too hard for both of them to handle.

The wind inside the wall was wet and thick and so heavy that they could not see anything. The wipers were going full speed, and they still couldn't see. They were at forty thousand feet, and the turbulence outside of the plane felt to them like the plane was going to be torn apart before too long. The altimeter reading was thirty thousand feet now, and ice started forming on the wings, and chunks of ice were hitting the plane. Some of the chunks were so big that you could feel the impact inside the plane. It felt so thick that it seemed like they were under water. There was hardly any difference between this and a slushy drink you get at the carnival. There was so much drag on the plane that they might stall at any moment, and their air speed was down to three hundred and fifty miles per hour. The temperature in the plane was thirty-three degrees. One more degree and they would become a Popsicle.

The altimeter read eighteen thousand feet, and it was falling fast. The air speed translated to four hundred miles per hour, and the air temperature began to rise. The ice turned to water, and the altimeter was ten thousand feet. The plane felt like a bucking bronco, and the air speed now read five hundred miles per hour. They could see light through the storm wall now, and the altimeter reading was four thousand feet and their air speed was 560 miles per hour.

When they broke through the wall of the storm at a thirty-degree angle, contentment turned to panic when they saw the water three to four hundred feet in front of them. They both pulled back on the stick with all their strength. As the plane evened out, they could see that they were only about fifty feet off the water. They looked at each other with a sigh and then simultaneously looked at the altimeter and couldn't believe their eyes.

The altimeter read sixteen hundred and fifty feet. Something was definitely wrong. This couldn't possibly be right. Tom tapped on the altimeter and nothing moved. They dismissed it and began to look around and discovered that the inside of the plane had about six inches of water in it.

Just then the engine began to sputter and cough. Tom reached over and turned off the oxygen. The engine straightened out and Tom flipped another switch for the water pump and the water began to leave the plane. They began to fly out into the middle of the storm.

It was rough and windy and hard to hold the plane level. Looking down at the water, there were these funny looking lines in the water. All of a sudden, Tom realized that Lydia was in the back and then Jerry looked back and saw her working frantically on the computer.

She looked up and said, "There is something definitely wrong here, guys. The water here is sixteen hundred feet above sea level, and those funny looking lines are current swells and they are moving about one hundred and twenty five miles per hour and getting slower toward the center of this thing. And if that isn't bad enough, there is a ship about two hundred and forty miles dead ahead."

Tom and Jerry looked at each other with bewilderment but didn't have time to react.

Lydia said, "If you think that's something, the last nine hundred feet of that storm wall we went through was 80 percent water at thirty-three degrees."

Jerry said to her, "Just where did you learn how?"

Lydia spoke before Jerry could finish his thought, "With my dad at NASA Weather! Now let's see just what is going on with that ship. See if you can call him on your radio."

Immediately, Jerry heard Tom talking to the ship captain. Captain Farrington, the ship's captain, was in a panic. He hadn't been able to contact anyone for the past twenty-two hours.

As Jerry looked out the window of the plane, it looked like a beautiful day in the opposite direction of the storm wall. Just how could he be in this horrendous situation where just hours ago he thought his life was over?

The captain reported to Tom on the radio that he had been steering a course of a circle for the past twenty-one hours. The currents were so strong that he had a hard time controlling his ship. The ship was a supertanker out of Hong Kong named the *Hong Kong Queen*. It had a full cargo of crude oil from Pakistan. She was holding her own on a fifty-mile circle. The captain was glad to hear Tom's voice. Did Tom have the heart to tell him what was going on?

"Captain, Sir, how did you get stuck in this storm?" Tom asked.

The ship's captain explained, "Tom, two days ago we were caught in the beginning of the hurricane. We had tried to get around it, but after twenty hours we hit a windstorm that turned us off course and we had to go with it to keep it from breaking us in two. After a few hours, there seemed to be this wall forming behind us and the current seemed to be getting stronger, so we went with the current and ten degrees away from the wall. As we got farther from the wall, the current was diminishing. So here we are twenty-two hours later and this thing looks like it is getting bigger."

"The wind down here is kind of funny," said the captain. "It is almost like it is moving upward. I have never encountered anything like it before."

"Does the wind seem to be getting stronger?" Tom asked.

"Yes," replied the captain. "The wind seems to be moving toward the wall and then going up. Do you have any idea of what this is and how I can get my ship out of here?"

"Well, this storm is not your ordinary storm, Sir," replied Tom. "Captain, sir, the storm you are in is just one of four storms and is the biggest of the four. I think this storm is a tornado, and it is about five hundred miles across. That's the good news. The bad news is there are three hurricanes outside of this tornado, and we think they are driving this tornado."

Then the captain asked, "Is there any way we can get out of here?"

"Well we're working on it, sir. Is everyone on board okay?" Tom asked.

The captain said, "Well yes, for right now, but we are all worried and tired."

Suddenly Jerry broke in. "Captain, do you know the current speed?

The captain replied, "Yes. The current speed is twenty knots, and we are moving about twenty-four knots. This overgrown tub never moved so fast. We are using starboard engine at three quarter speed and port at one-half speed. We seem to be holding our own."

Tom said, "How many on board?"

"Seventeen," the captain replied.

"Have you seen or heard from any other ships in this storm?" asked Jerry.

"Yes, just after we entered this storm, we heard from a sailboat by the name of *Play Toy*, a two-masted schooner. She was giving a distress call. I spoke to her skipper by the name of Bill Alberts for about five minutes. The *Play Toy* has a crew of three: Jack Thompson, Fred Roe, and Jeff Calsted. They were coming from Seattle and heading for Hawaii when they got caught in the storm. The skipper said that he has two grown children, Becky and Billy, who live in Portland, and would it be possible if we notified them of what is going on. Fred Roe has a sister living in Anchorage. The rest of the crew has no family. Skipper Bill Alberts explained to me that after traveling for only about ten miles that this wall looked like it was made of ice and the weather conditions changed drastically. He said the wind was blowing in the direction of the wall and up. The water current had changed and started to move toward the wall at a speed that is unbelievable. The wind and water drove them hard toward the wall. They had done everything a person can do to combat these conditions, but to no avail. Their forward mast was broken like a toothpick and had to be cut away to keep it from tearing them apart. The Skipper warned me to stay as far from this wall as possible because the waves that are hitting this ice wall are forty to fifty feet and it looks like nothing can survive. Then, all of a sudden, all I could hear was breaking up and ripping apart. I heard the skipper tell the crew to say their prayers because they were going down, and that was the last we heard," the captain said.

Captain Farington signed off, and after a silence, the radio broke with a voice.

"What in God's name are you doing down there, Tom? Over."

Tom answered, "Is that you, Gunner? Over."

Then the voice replied, "This is Captain William P. Gunnerson, US Coast Guard Hurricane Watch. How did you manage to get that old piece of junk into this mess? Over."

Tom replied, "I just had to make sure it was safe for you boys to come in. Over."

Gunner replied, "Well, how about telling us just what this great big overgrown critter is? Over."

Tom replied, "I don't think that I have ever seen anything the likes of this before. Looks like we got a supertanker in trouble, though. Over."

Gunner replied, "Say, are you guys going to stay in there all day or are you going to come out and tell us all about it over dinner? Over."

Tom replied, "Okay, why don't you talk to Captain Farrington and get the information you need so I can fly this little Caddy out of here. I'll meet you at the Jolly Roger tonight. Over."

Gunner replied, "Sure, good buddy, why don't you take that putt putt home and let the real eagles take care of everything here. Over."

Tom talked to the supertanker captain and introduced Captain Farington to Gunner over the radio and told him that they would contact the ship's owner and let them know their position.

As Tom flew over the supertanker, he turned his putt putt around, so to say, and began to climb. It was great! The plane was climbing so rapidly with the tailwind that they were at sixty thousand feet before they noticed that the engines were starving for air. When Tom turned on the oxygen, they were still fifty miles from the wall and climbing fast.

"At this rate, we will be in space before we reach the wall," said Tom.

Tom began to slow the plane's ascent but was still climbing. They were going so fast that he leveled the plane out, and it was still climbing but at a much slower rate. By the time they got to eighty thousand feet, the old bucket was straining pretty hard.

Tom called Gunner again. "Hey, Gunner, good buddy, how about giving me the coordinates on the northwest hurricane so I don't come out in the middle of it? Over."

"Sure thing, good buddy, thirty-five degrees north and 125 degrees west. And you will come out about fifty miles south of it. See you at the barn. Over," Gunner said.

So with the numbers Gunner gave them, they set a course and entered the wall and started their descent.

"What a ride!" Jerry said. "This time, we will not take such a steep descent, only one of about twenty-five degrees. We do not want to go through that ice again."

There was still the buffeting of the plane, the darkness, the rain and turbulence, but all and all, it was a little better this time. Tom and Jerry knew what to expect.

Lydia kept on the computers and stored a lot more information on the trip back through the storm. After all, what Jerry thought was a nightmare was in fact happening.

Jerry's thoughts rapidly shot back to his years in college.

Larry Walsh had been on everyone's lips in his weather class. Everyone knew him as a weather guru. Three times in Jerry's four years at UCLA, Larry Walsh had come to lecture on the weather and storm patterns. They knew that Larry Walsh had more knowledge than anyone on the planet, so his lectures where packed. If Lydia knew half as much as her father did about weather, then she would know as much as Tom or I do put together. I have to give it to her, the benefit of the doubt, that is. If we have to convince the weather people, we better be prepared. Lydia is a godsend. She has been a real trooper and has the ability to do the best job I have ever seen in my life. She knows as much about weather and computers as we do.

Now the altimeter read twenty thousand feet, and the plane was still tossing and buffeted like a toy. Tom, Jerry, and Lydia hadn't had much time to think of anything but this storm and how to survive it for the past five hours. They could now see light through the storm wall and realized that they were almost out of this critter.

I think this storm could make a believer out of anyone, thought Jerry.

Just then, they came out of the wall at about twelve thousand feet and went down to sea level to take a look at the trough, and there it was, just as Jerry had thought. The picture was complete in Jerry's mind, and now they headed for home.

Lydia spoke to Jerry, "What is so important about this trough anyway?"

Jerry said, "It is just the last piece of the puzzle that I have been putting together in my mind to finish this picture of the storm. All of the pieces fit exactly together, and there is no doubt left in my mind at all. This is my worst dream come true. This is the Colossus Tri-Hurricane Tornado Phenomena!

Tom broke in, "Are you sure?"

"Yes, I'm sure," Jerry said.

Lydia asked, "What does the trough have to do with it?"

Jerry explained, "The trough is caused by the tornado wall moving through the water at a high rate of speed and the suction of the water being pulled down under the wall and into the inside of the tornado. There is so much pressure from the water moving under the wall for four to five hundred feet and the entire circumference all around the five-hundred-mile diameter of the wall that the water has been pulled down below the sea level. This is all taking place just to pull the surface of the water that is being forced to move with the wall of the tornado down to flow into the inside of the storm."

Lydia said, "You mean that the water at the surface of the trough is moving as fast as the wall of the storm?"

"Yes, and as the water is being pulled by the wall, the water is also being sucked into the tornado with such force that it has left a void or has been pulled down from sea level to about one hundred feet below sea level and about five miles wide." Jerry sighed.

Tom spoke, "You mean that if you were in this trough, you would be pulled down under the wall and up into the inside of the tornado?"

Jerry said, "Hmmm, not quite. You would have to go down about fifty feet under the surface before that would or could happen. But to answer your question, yes, in that case you could. No one knows for sure because this has never happened before to our knowledge."

Tom said, "If the wall of the tornado is one to two thousand feet high in the air, then how can the bottom of the wall only be four to five hundred feet under the water? And shouldn't the wall be at least as deep as it is high?"

"I thought that when you put a piece of ice in the water only one third of the ice was out of the water?" Lydia said.

"That is true. However, in this case, the ice wall is moving at a high rate of speed from being powered by the three hurricanes, together with the force of the water being pulled under the wall at such a tremendous amount. Then you consider the centrifugal force of the water on the inside of the wall. Well all of these forces working together just overpower the weight of the wall of the tornado," Jerry replied.

"Well, what if one of the hurricanes leaves and goes somewhere else?" asked Lydia.

"Just pray that does not happen, because if it does, the wall will collapse and send a tidal wave out in every direction!" Jerry's voice shrieked.

The rest of the flight home was uneventful and smooth. Lydia and Jerry were on the computers and barely noticed the four-hour flight back until they landed and Tom was taxiing into the hanger.

Then Tom said, "We just have time to take a quick shower and change before meeting Gunner at the Jolly Roger."

Lydia didn't have a problem with that because she had just gotten back from a trip to Mexico and still had her bags in her car. They got into Tom's car and drove to Tom's place.

As they pulled into the parking lot of the Jolly Roger, Lydia could see her wounded and broken Caddy and thought to herself, *If Jerry hadn't run into me last night, I would not be on this great adventure.*

This has been the most exciting thing that has ever happened to me in my life.

Tom stopped the car at Lydia's instruction, and Lydia got out and opened the trunk of her rental car and took out one large suitcase and an overnight bag. Lydia put the bags in Tom's car and got in, and they drove to Tom's place.

Tom got into the shower first while Jerry and Lydia sat chatting in the office. Tom had just finished his shower and was dressed. He walked into the office, and turning to Lydia, he said, "The shower is down the hall to your left."

Lydia said, "Jerry, why don't you go first in the shower? I would like to call my dad."

Jerry did not argue with her. It had now been two days with very little sleep and no shower. The water was hot and very relaxing. Jerry took his time and let the hot shower rejuvenate him. After about twenty minutes, he felt almost human again and not tired. In fact, he felt ready to start all over again.

Lydia was on the phone with her dad all of the time that Jerry was in the shower. She told her dad how she had met Jerry Turner, the TV weather forecaster they had watched on the L.A. News for years before they moved to Florida. She explained to her dad how she had gotten into a fender bender with Jerry the night before in the parking lot and how she was okay and how she and Jerry had gone to the Jolly Roger, all about the receding water, and going to meet Tom next door. She explained how they had flown over Long Beach harbor and all the boats sitting on the sand and also how they had flown out into the storm and how Jerry seemed to know all about this gigantic storm. She told him how they were in the middle of the tornado and about the supertanker. Lydia told her dad about Captain Gunnerson of the US Coast Guard Hurricane Watch Plane and how they were going to have dinner with Captain Gunnerson at the Jolly Roger tonight. Lydia gave her dad a lot of details about the storm and Einstein's theory.

When Jerry got out of the shower, Lydia was still on the phone, so he finished dressing.

Lydia continued talking, "Dad, Jerry calls it Colossus Tri-Hurricane Tornado Phenomena. There are there hurricanes out there, but we could only see two of them and the biggest tornado that you could ever imagine. It is over five hundred miles across, and we flew right into the middle of it. There is a wall of solid ice that is about two thousand feet above sea level and about five miles thick, and it is moving. It is actually moving at a speed of 125 miles per hour. The tornado is actually what is sucking up the water from the ocean. On the inside of the tornado the water level is over sixteen hundred feet above sea level. Tom's plane is set up for weather watch and has five computers that we are able to obtain a mountain of information that we are making a report with. There are so many things to tell you about. Jerry seems to think that this storm could destroy the earth if it cannot be stopped in the next week or two. So what do you think, Dad?" Lydia said.

Larry said, "Jerry Turner is very knowledgeable about the weather and storms, so if he said this is Colossus Tri-Hurricane Tornado Phenomena, then on the surface I would tend to believe him. I will call Captain Gunnerson. After all, Gunner works for me. I will have him fly you and your party to Edwards Air Force Base tonight. In the meantime, I will set up a conference with the Joint Chiefs of Staff, the US military, and the president himself, along with the head of naval defense, the air force, Space Weather Tracking, the US coast guard, and the head of national defense. I will see you in the morning, honey! Try not to worry. We will sort all this out and do something about it in the morning. I love you, and I will see you tomorrow morning.

Lydia said good-bye and hung up the phone. Then she went to shower.

When Jerry was finished getting dressed, Lydia was already in the shower. Jerry walked into Tom's office.

Jerry picked up the phone and called Sandy in Montana, and after seven rings, Sandy answered the phone and spoke.

"Hello."

Jerry said, "Sandy, it's Jerry and I am sorry that I am calling so late but I told you I would call when I knew something. Are the boys and their families there with you?"

Sandy replied, "Well it is late and the boys and their families are here. We expected you to call before this."

Jerry said, "We just got back from the storm. It was a long flight, and we have been inside the storm and collected so much information, probably more then we really wanted. I have some bad news for you. Do you remember my midterm paper I wrote in college?"

Sandy said, "You mean that crazy theory that Einstein had?"

Jerry said, "Yes that one, but it is no longer a theory. It is the truth. We were in that storm today—you know, Colossus Tri-Hurricane Tornado Phenomenon!"

Sandy said, "Are you sure?"

"Yes," he replied.

Sandy said, "You mean it is the end of the world?"

Jerry replied, "Not if I have anything to say about it. Remember that I have been thinking about this storm and how to combat it for over twenty-five years, and I have a plan."

Sandy said, "Jerry just what can one man do? And how much time do we have?"

Jerry replied, "Now don't end the world just yet! Try not to be so negative and give us a week or two before you throw in the towel. Tell the boys that I love them and I will see them soon, okay?"

Sandy said, "Okay, and you be careful."

Jerry said, "I'll keep you informed of what is going on. Good-bye."

He hung up the phone.

Tom was working on the last of a series of pictures and diagrams when Lydia walked into the room after finishing her shower and getting dressed.

Tom turned to Jerry and said, "Can you believe this? This is like something out of a movie or novel, science fiction even! This is the hottest thing I have ever seen in my life!"

Tom was definitely excited. There was no doubt about that. They didn't have much time to get to the Jolly Roger, so they moved fast.

As they started for the Jolly Roger, Lydia said to Tom and Jerry, "I have talked to my dad, and he will make arrangements with Colonel Thompson at Edwards Air Force Base to get in touch with Gunner so that after dinner Gunner can fly us to Edwards Air Force Base for a joint conference with my dad, who is the head of NASA Weather in Florida. The Joint Chiefs of Staff, the US military, and the president himself will join this conference. Oh, and the head of naval defense, the air force and Space Weather tracking, US coast guard, and the head of national defense. Now, how's that for speedy action?"

Well to say the least, Tom and Jerry were shocked. Their chins must have hit the ground at least once.

They met Gunner at the Jolly Roger for dinner.

Tom introduced Lydia and Jerry to Gunner, and then they sat down to eat.

Gunner said to Lydia, "It is so good to finally meet you. I just talked to your dad on my way into Long Beach. I feel like I have known you all of your life. You see, I have known your dad for over thirty years. Not only is he one of my bosses, but he and I have been friends all of these years, and I have seen all of your pictures while you were growing up and going to college. It seems like I watched you grow up, and you have really impressed me with your accomplishments. Your dad and I served in two wars together."

Lydia interrupted, "Are you the same Gunner that saved my dad's life buy pulling him out of the water after he was shot down? I always wanted to meet you so I could thank you for saving my dad."

Gunner said, "When I was on my way in to Long Beach from the storm, your dad called and told me all about your phone call and the meeting at Edwards Air Force Base tomorrow. He asked if I would pick you and your party up and transport you to Edwards Air Force Base with me, and I said it would be my pleasure."

Naturally, after the day they all had, they were really hungry. During dinner, they filled Gunner in on what was really happening, and he gave them a report from NASA Weather. Gunner then told them that after dinner a car would pick them up to take the four of them to the airport, explaining that the head of the coast guard had called him before dinner and had given him orders to take them to Edwards Air Force Base.

CHAPTER 4

After boarding the US Coast Guard Weather Plane with Gunner and his crew, Jerry, Lydia, and Tom all sat in the back with the crew, four computer operators, a navigator, and two radar men. After takeoff, Gunner gave control to the co-pilot and found his way to the back, where Tom, Jerry, and Lydia were seated and sat down with them. Tom, Lydia, and Jerry had already begun to read the report Gunner had given them at the Jolly Roger.

The first thing in Gunner's report was the receding water of the coastline and how everything looked just as peculiar to him as it did to them. The coastline looked so unusual, it wasn't recognizable. The next thing in Gunner's report was the abnormal amount of icebergs in the water at this time of year, the breaking up of the Alaskan coast, and a very untypical icy water river flowing southward. The next thing in his report was about the speed of the river and the unusual swirls and whirlpools created by this fast-moving icy river. Then the observation of the largest iceberg that Gunner had ever seen was about halfway between Alaska and the storm. Gunner also reported the sighting of the Eskimo village as well as covered the enormity of the three hurricanes, but most of all, how gigantic the tornado in the center of the hurricanes was in comparison to the hurricanes.

Gunner and his crew had flown under the canopy of the tornado for about two hundred miles before they reached the wall of the tornado. At eighty thousand feet, they experienced the same turbulence and unstable air currents reaching over two hundred and twenty five miles per hour.

Because of their stronger horsepower and additional engines, they were able to fly straight through the wall of the storm without losing altitude. Gunner's US Coast Guard Hurricane Weather plane was equipped with all the latest computers and linked directly to the Navistar satellite systems. They were able to map the outline of all four storms and give a fair idea of just how big these storms were. His full report was much bigger, about eighty pages in all, but the report Tom, Lydia, and Jerry were reading was a condensed version.

At this point, Lydia took a seat directly in front of Jerry. He noticed her and smiled faintly. Lydia returned the smile. Gunner, sitting next to Jerry, asked about the ice in the wall of the storm, and the conversation continued on into the flight.

This is the report that the news media is broadcasting to the world, Gunner said. *These storms seem to be so big that we are having a hard time understanding them.*

On the local news, they heard a newsman report, "This storm is located thirty-five degrees north of the Equator in the North Pacific Ocean between the US and Japan. First, there are three hurricanes. Each hurricane is about one hundred miles across and in a triangle positioned to each other. In the middle of these three storms there is one gigantic storm. This storm looks like a tornado and is about five hundred miles across. The storm in the middle seems to be picking up the waters of the ocean like a funnel. It has been suggested that we use a nuclear device to stop this storm before it gets out of control! We will have more information in the morning."

"Well that does sound like they don't know very much at this time, and like always, they just want to destroy it because they don't understand what is going on," Jerry said, with disappointment in his voice. Jerry's eyes moved toward Lydia. He couldn't help notice how beautiful she was. It wasn't only in a physical sense, but she also had a sharp mind. Beneath it all, she had warmth and beauty of soul that was rare. Jerry was instinctively drawn to her, and it showed in the way he looked at her.

Again their eyes met. Lydia did not look away but tried to read what she saw in his eyes. She knew she was irresistibly drawn to him, though she could not understand why. She didn't ordinarily react that way to men, but Jerry was different. She seemed to find in him the embodiment of everything about her dad that appealed to her.

She saw in him everything that she dedicated her life to and could not help but to be powerfully drawn to him. She also knew he was attracted to her, and although his eyes left her, she continued to analyze him.

As Jerry looked up at Lydia, there was warmth. He felt a warming like the sun. He had never experienced anything like it.

Gunner broke the silence and said, "Well, they haven't got my report yet, and they need the satellite photos and computer data."

Just then Lydia spoke out with a frightened crackle in her voice, "Jerry, what are we going to do? I have been thinking about this storm, that it's too big and powerful for us to do anything about. Even if we do, the consequences to all of the coastal cities would be devastating. I have been very worried and frightened because I haven't been able to think of anything that could neutralize these storms. These reports, of atomic bombs and their devastating consequences, really have me worried, Jerry. Is there any way that life can go on like it used to be? Or are things going to change and be different for the rest of our lives?"

Jerry looked up at Lydia, wearing his heart on his sleeve, and knowing how worried she really was. He spoke to Lydia directly with a stern voice, "Lydia, maybe it's about time I tell you a little about my life."

Jerry started to explain not only for Lydia but also for Gunner and his crew. "I went to UCLA and majored in weather. All I could think of every minute that I was there was the weather and weather patterns, hurricanes, tornadoes, and storms. Because I majored in weather, my thesis was about a little-known fact. It had to do with Einstein. When I was a young boy, I read a lot of books about Einstein and his theories. I was very impressed, but there was this one theory that literally blew my mind. It was about storms—not just your ordinary storms but storms that were so out of proportion that they frightened me at that young age. This theory of Einstein's is called Colossus Tri-Hurricane Tornado Phenomenon. Now this theory that Einstein had could not be proven, but the concept was so good that I founded my entire thesis on the subject and received an A.

"Now I have done important research into the origins of various beliefs concerning the timing of the weather and storm patterns that cause big hurricanes and other storms. I knew that most of these beliefs had nothing to back them up. I always need proof to back me up. That's just how I am."

Lydia could see that everyone in the airplane was listening to every word that Jerry spoke. They were hanging on every word with this intense concentration. They wanted to know, just as Lydia did, what was going on and how they might be able to do something about the storm. Everyone on the plane seemed to think that Jerry had all the answers.

Jerry said, "Here is the theory Einstein had for the Colossus Tri-Hurricane Tornado Phenomena. If three hurricanes start close enough to each other and have enough cold air or water in a summer condition to react to each other, you know, like an air conditioning unit, they could cause a tornado to start in the center of the hurricanes. That could be more devastating than anything man has ever seen on this earth. His theory uses these three hurricanes as engines or motors, if you will, to power or run the tornado. In theory, when you take these three engines surrounding a tornado and add ice water, with air or water, it would act like a refrigerator to form ice."

Jerry spoke with a shaky voice. "I never expected to be able to prove Einstein's theory, but yesterday when we were going through the wall of the storm, there was no denying in my mind that Einstein knew exactly what he was talking about. This is Einstein's theory come to life—Colossus Tri-Hurricane Tornado Phenomena. Einstein did not have the technology that we have today. He had no answer to what we could do to combat this gigantic storm, nor did he even have any thoughts on what we could do to save ourselves. The only thing he left was his theory. Now I know that this doesn't sound very promising, but I haven't just thought about this for one or two days. I have been thinking about this for twenty years or better, and with the technology that we have today, I'm sure we can dissipate and bring this storm under control and probably even stop it completely. Actually, it's a very simple problem. The first thing that we have to do is to bring down the water level that is contained inside the wall of the tornado. This is the most dangerous part because we cannot destroy the integrity of the wall itself. If we do destroy the integrity of the wall, it will send a tidal wave that will destroy every coastal city it comes in contact with.

The second thing we need to do is to change the course of this icy cold water river that is flowing from Alaska and going directly into the storm. This is going to be very tricky, because the water must be out of the tornado before we change the course of the icy river. If we don't wait, it will destroy the integrity of the ice wall in the tornado that contains the water. If that happens, then, again, we will have a tidal wave. This can be done with the airplanes and missiles that we have today. We can be very precise in the delivery of this weaponry. We can drain the water out of the tornado and not cause any devastating problems to our coastal cities. We will have to have the cooperation of the government, the navy and all of our other armed forces if we are to succeed. I believe we can do it."

Jerry had conviction in his demeanor.

Lydia said, "Jerry, you are a godsend, and I believe in everything you have told us. I know that we are going to win over this storm, and I believe everyone on this plane agrees with me."

Just then, everyone on the plane began to clap and shout with Lydia. They gave praise to Jerry.

The atmosphere on the plane was very positive as Tom, Lydia, and Jerry filled Gunner in on their findings before they got to Edwards Air Force Base. It was the early part of the morning before sunrise in the upper desert of California.

When they landed, Colonel Frank Thompson, head of operations for Edwards Air Force Base, met them. He escorted them to the operations building where Lydia's father waited for them at a joint conference set up the night before. It was a big conference room complete with TV cameras and TV screens. There were tables with coffee and rolls where they spent the next hour waiting for things to get started. Just then, Lydia's father walked into the room.

Lydia screamed, *"Daddy!"* and ran to greet him.

Lydia brought her father over to meet Tom and Jerry. She introduced them, and they talked for a while. Her father noticed she had that twinkle in her eyes that he hadn't seen for many years when she spoke about Jerry, the look that only a father can see—a look of love and respect.

Lydia started to tell her father all about yesterday's mission and the storms. It seemed like she talked for hours before she took a breath of air.

"Wow," said her father. "It sounds like you had quite a trip in that storm, and it seems like you gathered more information in one trip then all of us could collect in a month. Where did you get such insight to these storms?"

"Daddy, Jerry wrote his thesis on this storm. He calls it 'Colossus Tri-Hurricane Tornado Phenomenon,' replied Lydia.

Larry asked, "Isn't that Einstein's theory that no one has been able to prove?"

"Until now, that is," interrupted Jerry. "What we saw yesterday morning, in my opinion, has proven to me that Einstein knew what he was talking about and what we are faced with. It is too big to describe without using the term biblical proportions."

"Jerry," Lydia's father said, "If you are right, then we are in big trouble, because Einstein gave us no clue on how to stop this enormous storm of yours."

"Daddy," Lydia said, "Jerry has thought of everything! We talked all about it on the way here. It sounds to me like we can stop this storm before it destroys us all. You have to convince the rest of our defenses that we can stop this storm. We don't have much time left before it is too late!"

Everyone had arrived at this time, so it was time to start.

A spokesman got up and asked everyone to please settle down and be seated.

"Ladies and gentlemen, I'd like to introduce to you the head of NASA Weather, Mr. Larry Walsh," the spokesman stated.

There was a roaring applause. Larry Walsh proceeded to the platform and motioned with his hand for everyone to quiet down.

"We will end the formalities and get to the point," said Larry. "You have the report by the coast guard weather plane and the reports of the latest satellite photos and computer data in front of you, but what you don't know is that we have three people here that were in the storm yesterday. They can tell us more then we want to know about these storms. So, without further ado, I give you Jerry Turner."

"Thank you, Larry," replied Jerry. "My good friends and peers, Lydia Walsh, Tom Goodman, and I, were in the storm yesterday in the North Pacific Ocean. I would like to take this time to bring you up to date with this situation and the enormity of the problem we have at hand."

Jerry took a moment to clear his thoughts and look around the conference room and then continued.

"A single thunderstorm can release 150 million gallons of water, and a full-blown hurricane will multiply that by twelve thousand. With 125 mile per hour winds, it can devastate most anything. When volatile air masses collide or otherwise interact, storms sweep across the earth's surface and can vent their fury around the earth. The storms are vital as the earth's engine and work as air conditioners, continually exchanging warm air from the tropics for cool air from the Polar Regions. But up until now, there has been no need for concern because these storms have not joined forces. The storm we have here is so big that you will have a hard time understanding it, so open your mind as much as you can."

Jerry looked through the crowd to try and get a feel of the reaction in people's faces.

"This storm is located thirty-five degrees north of the Equator in the North Pacific Ocean between the US and Japan at longitude one hundred and seventy degrees. First there are three hurricanes; each hurricane is about one hundred miles across and in a triangle adjacent to each other. Each is turning in a clockwise direction, and in the middle of these three storms there is one gigantic storm that is turning in a counterclockwise direction. This center storm is being powered by the three hurricanes like three powerful engines feeding the storm on the inside. This storm looks like a tornado, but in biblical proportions. The bottom of this storm or funnel is approximately five hundred miles across, and the sides or walls extend to the sky five to ten miles. The top of the funnel looks to be one thousand miles across, towering over the hurricanes like they were toys. Again, the three hurricanes are the power source of the tornado. Now from the North Pole, there is an icy flowing river streaming in to this storm. From satellite view, this ice flow is so pronounced that it seems that we should have seen it days ago. There is something so terribly wrong here that this could possibly be the beginning of the end of the Earth as we know it! I don't want to frighten you, but you all should be concerned. Now I'll be taking questions."

"Are we to understand that you think that this storm could destroy the Earth?" a reporter belted out.

"If this storm continues, yes!" said Jerry.

"Now to understand this better, you have to know just what this storm is doing and how it is doing it! These storms are not moving in any direction because the center storm is pulling into its core vast amounts of water. By this time, inside the core, the water level is more than eighteen hundred feet above sea level. The only thing that is keeping the water from collapsing out of the core is that the wall of the tornado has turned to ice and created a vacuum on the inside of the center tornado that is sucking up water at an enormous rate. The wall of this tornado is about five miles thick and getting thicker by the hour."

Jerry looked at Lydia as if to say, "Am I doing all right?" with sweat running down his forehead. Jerry pulled out his handkerchief from his back pocket and wiped his forehead. Looking at Lydia again, Jerry could see her smiling at him and was reassured that everything was going fine.

"It has been suggested that we use a nuclear device to stop this storm! Please stop and consider the consequences of this suggestion. If we destroy the integrity of the walls of this storm, it will send a wall of water eighteen hundred feet high around the world two or three times and destroy the coastal cities as we know them today. That would be at best. Now there is a trough at the base of the walls of the tornado that seems to be at least five miles across and about fifty to one hundred feet deep that is moving counterclockwise with the wall of the tornado. They are all moving at a speed of over 125 miles per hour. Now to understand this better, the wall of the tornado is about two thousand feet of solid ice and slushy ice to about twenty five thousand feet," said Jerry.

Then there came a break in the conversation when Houston's command broke in with news from the shuttle.

"We have a problem; we just passed over the Atlantic Ocean and are now over Chicago. It must be sunrise in California and still dark over the Pacific Ocean. In the blackness of the horizon we can see something that we have never seen before. It looks like the earth's canopy or ozone layer is puffing outwardly. This is in the location of the storms that are being investigated. From where we are right now, we can't see the storms, but it should be sunrise by the time we get to that location. By our estimation, this puffing looks to be pushed out about five to ten miles higher than the earth's canopy and about one thousand miles across. The blackness of space behind the earth makes it clear from this vantage point but we have never seen anything like this before. Could someone tell us just what is going on here? This is Houston. We'll keep you up to date, and we'll break in when we have more information, over."

"Are there anymore questions?" asked Jerry.

Many of the people raised their hands, and he answered their questions. Lydia's mind wandered to how she loved the way Jerry handled people. He answered each person's question in a different way, as if he understood what each needed to hear, and each one responded accordingly. His mastery of the dynamics of this storm, in which he gracefully seemed to empathize with the people's anguish, brought people some form of peace inside. The very simplicity of his understanding of the storm she found unsettling. As she thought of him, she couldn't help but wonder what his personal life was like. What did he do when he went home on any other given day? Was it an empty house without anyone there to talk to? Was he lonely? What did he think of in the quiet of his thoughts in that empty house? Jerry had told her that he was divorced and lived alone. Would he be terribly upset if she came to visit him some evening after he finished his work? Looking up at Jerry, their eyes met and she felt he could read her thoughts, and she blushed. But his smile also seemed to say to her, "Come on over." And in her heart, she answered, "Okay."

When the questions were finished, Jerry explained, "I do have a plan that I believe will work. The wall of the storm is at least five miles thick, and we cannot penetrate that much ice without breaking the walls up with a single blast. So I suggest that we make a hole through the ice with a series of blasts guided by a laser that will guide the missiles to different depths until we break through the five miles of ice. This hole should be at an angle at ten degrees up from the base of the wall and a thirty-degree angle in the direction that the tornado is moving. So when the hole is open, the water will come out behind and down from the direction of the tornado and lay down in the trough as the wall moves. This should be done in three different places at the same time in between the hurricanes. I think that this can be done with nuclear subs to deliver the laser for guidance and missiles for the blasts. Each missile will follow the last into the hole until it passes through the entire wall. This could take at least twenty missiles per hole. I don't know the particulars of this, but the air force or navy will have the answers for us. If the blasts are successful, the storm should drain in one or two days.

"Now, there are a lot of details to work out, so we better get started. Thank you, ladies and gentlemen."

Jerry left the platform, and Larry Walsh walked back up.

"We should be proud of Jerry, Tom, and Lydia for their heroism for going into the storm and bringing back such valuable information. And now that we have most of the facts, we should be able to make a quick and speedy decision. Mr. President, I know that the head of defense is with you at this time, and I strongly recommend that you give the orders to proceed as quickly as possible. Thank you. This meeting is on hold until further notice," said Mr. Walsh

Colonel Frank Thompson, head of operations at Edwards Air Force Base, came to their group after the meeting to tell Tom, Jerry, and Lydia that he had made arrangements for them to stay in some little houses on base. He realized that they were very tired by this time. The cars were outside to take them to their quarters.

Colonel Thompson explained that if there was any news he would wake them up and fill them in.

The colonel had assigned two cars and ordered them to be on standby in the event that Tom, Jerry, or Lydia needed anything. It only took about ten minutes to get to their quarters. There were five little houses nestled in a clump of trees on a small hill just far enough away that you could not hear the commotion of the airstrip. They were quaint and roomy two-bedroom cottages and very nicely decorated. Lydia's cabin was next door to Tom and Jerry's cabin. Larry, Lydia's father, stayed behind. He had a good night's sleep on the plane from the cape to Edwards.

As they arrived at their quarters, there was food and a change of clothes waiting for them. Jerry remembered the colonel had said if they needed anything, all they had to do was ask and it would be supplied. He assured Jerry that it would take at least three to four hours before there would be any news and that Jerry, Tom, and Lydia should get some rest because it looked like this would be a long battle.

It was just before 10:00 a.m. when Jerry showered, shaved, and fell asleep within twenty minutes. Tom was sleeping by the time Jerry got out of the shower. Lydia was in her own little house fast asleep.

Now while they were sleeping, conferences were going on all over the United States. Senator Blackman from Tennessee had joined together with a Colonel Rogers of the Strategic Air Command and other powerful men in the government and in the Armed Forces. These men were advocating the use of an atomic bomb to destroy the storm and not to spend millions or billions of the taxpayers' money.

They were the kind of people who didn't think of the consequences because they only thought of money, position, and power. They thought of how they could position themselves in the future. It didn't matter to them what the cost to mankind. These men had already launched an attack through the news media and throughout the world. These men were powerful in the press and in the news media. They had the press convinced that there was no danger and it could be all over in a matter of minutes by the use of an atomic blast.

Colonel Rogers and Senator Blackman contacted Colonel Frank Thompson, head of operations at Edwards Air Force Base.

"Colonel Thompson, sir, please join in with our efforts to squash this all out battle against a storm that can't possibly hurt anyone," stated Senator Blackman.

"The expenses for this operation could possibly take away from money that would normally be spent in the direction of the Edwards Air Force Base. You could be made a laughingstock of the country and in fact the world if your efforts do not pan out."

For thirty minutes, he tried reasoning with Colonel Thompson that it would be a losing battle. They did everything short of threatening him to get him to join forces with them. Colonel Rogers and Senator Blackman tried to convince Colonel Thompson that the news media was blasting the president of the United States and the congress, along with the joint chiefs of staff, for not doing something immediately. They were accusing them of trying to spend taxpayers' money on a big fiasco. Colonel Thompson listened to them, but somehow he didn't quite believe what they were saying and decided to keep an eye on them. Colonel Rogers and Senator Blackman just could not let it go, so they called their own conference with many powerful men who were heads of states and heads of other countries.

Meanwhile at the White House, the president and his cabinet had been bombarded by scientists, diplomats, and heads of countries from all over the world reminding them that they had an agreement with them not to use nuclear weapons. If they used nuclear weapons on this storm, it would be considered an act of war. Most of the countries of the world had agreed on this and stood fast together. These powers included the USSR, Japan, China, Africa, Great Britain, and all of the nations of the U.N.

At 11:00 a.m., Colonel Rogers of the Strategic Air Command and most of the powerful men at the conference made their own decision. At 11:25, Colonel Rogers made his one fatal decision to divert a B-52 bomber that was flying over the USSR to head for the storm. The B-52 was carrying two bombs with atomic war heads. Colonel Rogers knew his decision could end his career in the air force if it turned bad.

At 11:30 a.m., Colonel Thompson was notified by NORAD and the NAVSTAR System of the change of course and destination of the B-52.

At 11:40 a.m., Colonel Thompson called the president to inform him of just what had happened in the past forty minutes, and Colonel Rogers' actions in diverting the B-52.

At 11:45 a.m., Colonel Rogers received a call. "This is the president of the United States, and I am calling you to give you a direct order.

"I want you to get on the radio and contact that B-52 and order it to turn around and get it back on its original course.

"Do you understand me, Colonel Rogers?"

"Yes, Mr. President," Colonel Rogers said.

Colonel Rogers gave the order for the B-52 turn around and return to its original course.

CHAPTER 5

As Jerry, Lydia, and Tom slept, this single act by Colonel Rogers would become one of the deciding factors in the president's decision to back Jerry Turner's plan to combat the storm.

It was 4:00 p.m. when Jerry woke up and looked out of the window to see the hot afternoon sun. He poured himself a cup of coffee and sat down at the table to reflect and absorb what had happened in the past forty or so hours. People baffled him. He thought they found it so difficult to be broad-minded or to open their minds to see another point of view. They grasped so persistently to things of their teaching, which they never dared to question. To hold to one's reliance is one thing, but to hang on to mere established practices that do not really push the envelope of enlarging one's mind to accept the unknown and to observe and explore so that you can invent the solution to a problem is mere suicide.

As Jerry finished his first cup of coffee, there was a tap on the door. He went to answer it and was stunned to see Lydia standing there. She looked striking in her flatteringly fit silk dress. It was light summer blue, was soft and sheer, and accentuated her sleek figure. Jerry's mood changed as soon as he saw her. His face relaxed and lit up with a broad smile. The two of them embraced lightly, and he invited her in.

Jerry was glad she had come over and offered her a cup of coffee. He was fond of Lydia and knew that she liked him. He needed the comfort of a friend. It had not been a pleasant two days, and Jerry could clearly see the way things were going.

The future seemed bleak, and her coming over was a welcome relief from the tension of the past two days and helped to ease the tension and gloom that had overtaken him.

As far as the weather was concerned, Jerry and Lydia had a lot in common. She was deeply involved in weather conditions and had so many questions to ask Jerry. She was probably not at all aware of how she really felt about him, and even though she may have originally been drawn to him for purely platonic reasons, each hour the attachment became more intense. She found herself thinking about him in the last forty hours and asking herself how he would feel about this or that and wishing she could talk to him about it, but all they talked about was this plan or that idea. Since the storm was more important than both of them, the only way she would ever be able to enter into any kind of a relationship with him was if they could stop this thing. When she saw how happy he was to see her, she was glad she had come over to see him.

"Jerry, I hope you don't mind my barging in on you this way," Lydia said in a halfhearted apology.

"Not at all," replied Jerry. "In fact, nothing seems to be going right in the last two days, and I was feeling down. I'm glad you came over. In fact, you have already lifted me up."

"After knowing you for only a short time," said Lydia, "I find that you are an intense person. You have so many different opinions and ideas on the weather and these storms that it is a breath of fresh air. I value your opinions and the unique viewpoint you express. My own work is very demanding, and I am asked for my opinion on a variety of topics relating to people's opinions and their relations to each other. As I have watched you relate to other people, it seems so easy for you to flow with their feelings to give them comfort. It is an art, you know! I don't feel adequate sometimes and only wish I could discuss some of these matters with you in a much deeper manner. I know you could offer valuable suggestions."

Jerry replied, "When we get through this storm business, maybe we can talk more about our own lives in a more relaxed atmosphere."

Lydia suddenly felt more at ease.

"This little house looks like something you would live in, being a bachelor and all," Lydia said. "I mean, it's a perfect setup, although it does look a lot too simple for a man as complex as you."

She continued trying to get Jerry to loosen up so he would reveal something about himself.

"It could be all I really need and would serve a purpose in a practical way. I don't spend much time in the house anyway, so I don't need a lot. My dreams go a lot further than a house and these four walls," Jerry said playfully.

"You really dream?" Lydia said.

"Of course, doesn't everyone?" said Jerry.

"What do you dream about?" she replied.

"About people I meet, about things I would like to accomplish," Jerry said.

"Did you dream today? And was I in any of your dreams?" Lydia asked.

Jerry smiled warmly. "Yes, I thought of you today, and I respect so many things about you. You have many gifts and a beauty that is beyond compare."

Lydia had been hoping that he would say something like that, and when he did, she blushed lightly and replied, "I feel the same way about you, and I hope that we can get to know each other better when this storm is over."

Just then the phone rang, and Jerry answered it. It was Colonel Thompson, and he was sending the car to pick them up. Lydia started walking to the door.

Jerry followed, saying to her, "Thank you for your visit. It picked up my spirit."

As they were standing at the door, Lydia turned toward Jerry and tilted her head slightly, offering him an opening if he wanted to kiss her. Jerry placed his hands on her shoulders and . . . just then Tom called out from the bedroom. "Who was that on the phone?"

Tom entered the room.

Jerry kissed her warmly on the cheek. She responded, embracing him, and kissed him affectionately on the cheek.

Jerry turned to Tom and said, "That was the colonel, and he is sending the car to pick us up, I'm going to walk Lydia to her door. I'll be right back."

The car arrived to pick them up, and Tom got in the car, as Jerry waited for Lydia in the hot and dry afternoon sun. Lydia ran out of the little cottage and slipped in the backseat with Tom, and Jerry slipped in behind her as they started the ten-minute drive to headquarters.

"It looks very dry out there in the desert," Tom said.

Lydia added, "Not quite like it was yesterday over the Pacific. It was beautiful and clear, bright, and a little stormy, plus we almost became Popsicles in that storm."

Lydia chuckled.

Jerry said, "The desert is most precious in the spring. Everything is in bloom and quite beautiful."

"Leave it to you to find the best in everything," said Tom.

When they arrived at the conference hall, Colonel Frank Thomson met them. He began to fill them in on just what was going on during the time they had been asleep. The news media had the whole world up in arms. Senator Blackman and Colonel Rogers of the Strategic Air Command and other powerful men in the government had joined forces to stop Tom, Jerry, and Lydia's efforts to battle the storm. Colonel Thompson explained to them how most of the countries of the world had joined forces and been in contact with the president of the United States. Most other countries of the world had told the president that if the United States used nuclear weapons on the storm, it would be a declaration of war. Colonel Thompson apologized to Tom, Lydia, and Jerry for not allowing them more than five hours of sleep, but in his words, this place had been a madhouse, buzzing like a beehive, and no one seemed to know what to do next.

Larry Walsh and Colonel Thompson were both in agreement that what was needed more than ever was levelheaded thinking and a take charge attitude.

Larry Walsh added, "From the time you, left I have been on the phone with several influential scientists and theorists from around the world, and the overwhelming opinion is that they corroborate with Jerry's conclusion of Einstein's theory. An hour ago, I heard from the Scientific Research Association, and 95 percent of the scientists believe that your plan has a 99 percent chance of success and the only plan that takes into consideration life and property. I have just gotten off the phone with the president of the United States. I gave him all of the evidence from the scientific community around the world. The president has gotten the same reaction from congress, the joint chiefs, the cabinet, and the military services. I explained to him your findings, the coast guard's, the satellite, and the shuttle results. All these things add up to just one answer.

"Colonel Thompson and I are in agreement that your plan is the only logical and life-saving plan that there is. The deciding factor happened earlier today when you were sleeping. Colonel Rogers of the Strategic Air Command and others screwed up by diverting a B-52 bomber that was flying over the USSR with two bombs that had atomic warheads aboard. Colonel Rogers and other powerful men thought they could secretly divert the B-52 to stop the storm. If I had not found out about it, then it would already be too late. I called the president, and he called Colonel Rogers and put a stop to it.

"Diplomats from countries all over the world have been up in arms over this and have been threatening the United States with war. The president, the joint chiefs of staff, the cabinet, and the entire military services have joined together to back your plan. Jerry, he will back you with all of the military forces of the United States. In ten minutes, the president of United States will go on the world—wide media services, TV, and radio to announce to the world that you, Jerry Turner, have been given full control and authority over all military services involved. The code name given to this operation is Storm Safe. After the president's announcement, you will be introduced to the world media by the president himself, at which time you can tell the world what has been going on, what this storm is all about, and how you intend to stop this storm with a minimum amount of human loss."

Jerry was flushed and white with embarrassment. He could hardly catch his breath and hardly knew what to say.

Then Jerry thought to himself, *What if I am wrong? What if Einstein was wrong and this isn't what I think it is? What if I fall and make a mistake? What if this doesn't work? What about all the people who are depending on me? Will I make a fool of myself?*

Lydia could see that Jerry felt troubled, and she sensed that there must be a flood of thoughts going through his mind, so she walked over to Jerry and put her arm around him to reassure him. She said to him quietly, "Jerry, we're all behind you, and not only do we believe in you, but we know you're right."

Then Tom spoke out and said, "That's okay, Jerry, you know you have been right since the first day of high school. This storm is exactly what you said it is. You know the proper way to take care of this storm. There is no one here who isn't on your side and won't back you all the way."

Larry Walsh interrupted Tom and said to Jerry, "I have read all the reports from the coast guard, the news, the satellites, and the shuttle, and I feel that you are more on target with these storms than anyone on this earth. You have my full backing."

Just then there was a silence in the room. The president of the United States walked in and proceeded to the platform.

The announcer spoke, "Ladies and gentlemen, the president of the United States."

The president started speaking. "I only have two points to make this morning. Number one is that I am declaring a state of emergency and invoking martial law in all major cities in the United States, and I am ordering the national guard, army, and marines into action immediately. My second point is that I assure you that a decision has been made. My cabinet, the war department, the chiefs of staff, all of the armed services, and the NASA Weather Bureau have made the right decision. Our decision to fight this storm on its own ground is based on the desire to save coastal cities of the world from mass destruction. There is one man in our country who knows more about these storms and has shed more light than any weather bureau or satellite or even the coast guard has been able to do. This man, with two others, has been in the storm and has gathered more data and information than all of our agencies had been able to collect in the past three days. It gives me great pleasure to introduce to you the man I have put in charge over the Storm Safe Operation, Mr. Jerry Turner. Mr. Turner?"

As Jerry stood at the podium at Edwards Air Force Base in California after being introduced by the president of United States, he was speechless for a moment. Then Jerry spoke, "Thank you Mr. President. All my thanks go to the war department, the chiefs of staff, and all of the armed services. And also to the weather bureau at NASA and a special thanks to Larry Walsh the head of NASA Weather and to Colonel Frank Thompson here at Edwards Air Force

Base, who has been very kind and gracious and instrumental in my appointment to this position.

"Yesterday, my very good friends, Tom Goodman and Lydia Walsh, and myself flew in to this storm in Mr. Goodman's plane. We flew through the wall of the main storm and were able to gather an enormous amount of information. Since yesterday morning, we have been sharing information with NASA Weather, the news media, the coast guard, and every service that has a need. With all the information that has been gathered through satellite, shuttle, and coast guard weather planes, storm-tracking ships, and even our small plane, we have been able to come up with a plan that we believe will take the danger out of these storms and eventually stop them in a matter of days. I don't have much more to say today, so I will turn this conference over to Colonel Frank Thompson at this time. Thank you. Colonel?"

"Thank you, Jerry," replied Colonel Thompson. "We will give you more information as it comes in. Now that we are off worldwide broadcasting, we will continue on our own closed secret security station. All of you here have security clearance, with the exception of Jerry, Lydia, and Tom. Hereafter, by order of the president of the United States, a special top-security clearance is granted. After a short briefing, we will continue."

The short briefing was held by Larry Walsh, who explained briefly to Lydia, Jerry, and Tom just what had happened. Then Larry Walsh nodded to Colonel Thompson to continue.

Colonel Thompson introduced Admiral John L. Norstrum. Admiral Norstrum thanked Colonel Thompson and then began to explain the complement of ships and planes that would be used in Operation Storm Safe.

"The following are the submarines that have been decided on and chosen to go to the storm," said Admiral Norstrum. "The first of the Ohio-class boats is the USS *Georgia* SSBN-727, commanded by Captain Earl W. McCrary. It is a nuclear-powered submarine with a complement of fifteen officers and one hundred and forty-two rating seaman.

"The second of the Ohio-class boats is the *Tennessee* SSBN 734 commanded by Captain John Howard Towers. It is a nuclear-powered submarine with the same complement.

"The third of the Ohio-class boats is the *Alabama* SSBM 738 commanded by Captain Robert R. Spencer. It is a nuclear-powered submarine with the same complement.

"The fourth is of the Los Angeles-class boats, the USS *Honolulu* SSN-718, commanded by Captain Todd T. Tarance and Admiral John L. Norstrum, commander of operations. It also is a nuclear-powered submarine with a complement of twelve officers and one hundred and twenty-seven rating seaman.

"The fifth is of the Seawolf-class boats and is the highly classified USS *Seawolf* SSBN-22 commanded by Captain Richard P. Batington. It also is a nuclear-powered submarine. It has a complement of twenty officers and one hundred and fifty-six rating seaman.

"The sixth is of the Seawolf-class boats. Its name is the USS *Mississippi* SSBN-24 commanded by Captain Blain Boyd Bates III. It is a nuclear-powered submarine and has the same complement.

"The seventh is of the Seawolf-class boats. Its name is the USS *Washington* SSBN-26 commanded by Captain Ernest L. Gunther. It is also a nuclear-powered submarine and has the same complement.

"These are the ships we picked for project Operation Storm Safe. All have been fitted with precision-guided laser systems that can guide missiles into and through a five-mile hole in the ice of the wall of the storm.

"The boats will be paired up in three positions, one hundred and twenty degrees from the center of the storm and each other, approximately two hundred miles from the center of the storm. The first pair will be the USS *Georgia* SSBN-727 and the USS *Seawolf* SSBN-22. The second pair will be the USS *Tennessee* SSBN-734 and the USS *Mississippi* SSBN-24. The third pair will be the USS *Alabama* SSBN-738 and the USS *Washington* SSBN-26. We're also using the aircraft carriers USS *Abraham Lincoln* CVN and the USS *Enterprise* CVN, both out of Alameda, California.

"The command staffs on board the Aircraft Carrier USS *Nimitz* CVN include: Commander Naval Air Force, US Pacific Fleet; Commander Third Fleet; Commander Anti-Submarine Warfare Wing; Aircraft Carrier USS *Constellation* under command of Captain Lester L. Larson; Aircraft Carrier USS *John F. Kennedy,* Commander Billy J. Bates; Aircraft Carrier USS *Ticonderoga*, Commander Harlo

P. White, US Pacific Fleet; and Commanders, Carrier Groups One and Seven.

"Commander Naval Air Force, US Pacific Fleet Vice Admiral Edwin R. Kingston is the direct representative of and the principal advisor to the commander in chief, US Pacific Fleet for operations, support, and administration of naval aviation in the Pacific. His primary mission is to oversee all Pacific naval air units and develop their operational readiness and combat abilities so this mission falls under the protection of the United States. His area of responsibility covers the west coast of North America to Japan, from pole to pole. His main responsibility is the protection of the western sea as it approaches to the United States. He will report directly to the president all data pertaining to Operation Storm Safe. All aircraft have been made ready and are at standby condition."

Colonel Thompson said to Jerry, "In all my years, I have never seen a better battle plan than that which you have presented to us as a solution to the storm. I know I speak for all the armed services throughout the United States when I say we will back you all the way. Everyone I have been in contact with, including the president of United States, is with you 100 percent. The chiefs of staff and the war department have commented that this is the best they've ever seen."

Lydia and her father, along with Tom and Gunner, were all patting Jerry on the back and congratulating him.

Vice Admiral Edwin R. Kingston stepped forward and gave the orders for all naval personnel to report to their ships immediately. The order was given to all ship captains to make ready to put out to sea. Storm Safe would be the biggest peacetime operation ever in the history of the United States.

Every freighter, frigate, tug, battleship, destroyer, and carrier—every ship that can float on the West Coast of the United States was ordered to sea.

Most of the combat aircraft that are stationed on the carriers are Grumman F-14 Tomcats. They qualify to lay claim to being one of the world's most potent interceptors that the navy has in their array on board their carriers and can carry four sparrow missiles and four sidewinder missiles. The carriers were commanded to stay two hundred miles from the wall of the storm with squadrons of four F-14 Tomcats and four F18 Hornets. They would take off every ten minutes to deliver their payload to the target. Helicopter combat support squadrons would be on site, and so would the Apaches and Sea Kings. The E-2C Hawkeye airborne early warning airplanes would be in the air at all times.

The submarines were twenty-five miles from the wall of the storm in position and ready when Admiral Kingston gave the order to start Operation Storm Safe from the carrier *Nimitz*. The subs were positioned behind one of the hurricanes at the edge of the trough moving away from the hurricane and about three hundred miles from the next one and two hundred fifty miles from the center of the storm. Admiral Norstrum, aboard the USS *Honolulu*, gave the command to the submarines to start into the trough.

Captain McCrary gave the order from the operations room to go ahead! The submarine began to go over the edge of the trough and descend. Immediately the boat began to toss and buck with the force of the speed of the water. The sub was almost out of control. The captain ordered, "Maximum speed!" The boat began to pitch and roll to the left toward the bottom of the trough. The captain ordered all hands to man their stations, and for the next ten minutes, they felt like a surfboard riding a big wave shooting to the bottom of the trough. The laser was mounted on the communications tower, so they could not dive to get more control and had to ride it out.

Meanwhile, on the USS *Tennessee*, Captain Towers was having the same problems trying to keep control of his boat as it approached the bottom of the trough. They could hear the wind on the inside of the boat and could hear pieces of ice hitting the hull as they passed by as if they were going backward.

The captain of the *Alabama*, Robert Spencer, was not having such good luck. His boat felt like it was breaking up, and as he reached the bottom of the trough, the boat started up on the other side.

Captain Spencer and his crew were in trouble, and the boat was leaking like a sieve. The back of the boat was trying to come around. They started to lose control. The captain ordered his crew to turn the rudder halfway to the right, and the boat did not respond. The captain ordered his crew to turn the rudder three-quarters of the way to the right, and the boat started to turn and head down to the bottom of the trough. As they got to the bottom again, they swung upward, away from the wall of the storm. The captain ordered the crew to turn the rudder halfway to the left, but it was too late because the centrifugal force had began to throw them out of the trough like a toy, and within five minutes they had been thrown out and found themselves trying to regroup. Now the captain ordered the boat back into the trough, and it started all over again, only this time it seemed to be rougher than before.

Captain Towers had ordered the ballast tanks filled to get more stable and to try to get the laser ready for targeting. The control of the boat was so bad that the captain told the admiral that it did not look good. The boat started moving at about one hundred miles per hour, and the steering was almost impossible. The water was pushing the stern like a tail wind. The admiral told the captain to try more ballast and to pull the bow of the boat up to try to get more control. The admiral told Captain Towers that they had a fifteen-minute window to get the job done.

Just then, Captain Spencer broke in with a, *"Mayday!"* The sub was in a crash dive condition. They were being pulled under the wall of the storm with the boat leaking, pitching, rolling, shaking, and bouncing like it was going to tear apart any minute. The first mate told Captain Spencer that the temperature was getting close to freezing, and they began to hear ice chunks hitting the hull all through the boat. Reports from forward compartments stated that everything was freezing, and now it sounded like they were going through gravel, as if the sound was like sandpaper on the hull. Captain Spencer ordered an emergency dive procedure. The sub was at 250 feet and diving deeper. The controls were very sluggish and did not respond very fast. There were big chunks of ice hitting the hull, and everyone was worried and trying every trick that they knew.

"We are approaching three hundred and twenty five feet and still diving at thirty degrees down bubble," replied the captain on his transmitter.

The sound was deafening.

The boat seemed to be beginning to break up. There were reports from forward and aft of leaking and stress on the hull.

The pumps forward were all overloaded, and they started taking on more water than they could get rid of. They just hit four hundred feet, and now they faced a new problem. The sub's speed had increased to 180 miles per hour. It felt like a roller coaster going down the first fall, and their depth reached 420 feet.

It grew silent for a moment, and then the first sound Admiral Norstrum heard on his radio was, *"Oh no*, it feels like the bottom of a roller coaster when you make that curve to start going up. And now we are being shot upward like we are being shot out of cannon. Our speed is over two hundred and twenty-five miles per hour. The noise and pressure are so bad we don't think the boat can take much more. But wait a minute, we are slowing and it is beginning to get smoother. Our speed is only one hundred and eighty miles per hour. The pitching and bucking is less now, and our bubble is up twenty degrees. Our speed has slowed to one hundred and forty miles per hour. It is slowing even more now, and the boat is beginning to move toward the surface. It is beginning to get smoother, and our speed is down to one hundred miles per hour now. We are at sea level.

"We are going up fast one thousand feet above sea level now. And now we are at one thousand two hundred feet above sea level and rising. Things are smoothing out more and more.

"The further we're going up, the better and smoother the boat is, and now we have some kind of control over the boat. That's if you consider this control. We are at one thousand five hundred feet above sea level now and still rising. Damage control has reported in, and we have everything under control now that we have stopped all the leaks. The hull is standing up very well, and fire control has just reported that all are in good shape. We are at one thousand seven hundred and twenty-five feet above sea level. The bubble is up at thirty degrees and rising fast. Our speed is just over one hundred miles per hour and holding. There is only one casualty. Midshipman Peterson broke his left arm when we went under the wall. Now we are at one thousand nine hundred feet above sea level and still rising. We have just surfaced at two thousand and sixty five feet and our speed has dropped to seventy-two miles per hour. We have some control now. Surface team is going topside and will give us a report in a few minutes. Things have leveled out considerably, and we have just started to get comfortable. The boat is at one forth left rudder, and we are moving toward the center of the storm slowly.

"The report from topside is that we are about forty miles from the wall of the storm and conditions are rough, cloudy, and the wind is at fifty miles per hour and is moving upward. We have radar contact with the tanker and are about to have radio contact momentarily."

Admiral John Norstrum made the decision to pull out the 727 boat *Georgia* and the 734 boat *Tennessee* from the trough before the same thing happened to them. Then he ordered the USS *Seawolf* with Captain Batington and the USS *Mississippi* with Captain Bates and the USS *Washington* with Captain Gunther, the three newest and fastest nuclear-powered submarines, into the trough.

As they went over the side of the trough, they all experienced the same sensation of feeling like a surfboard riding a big wave to the bottom of the trough. All three captains experienced the same things as the other captains in the older subs—the tossing, rolling, bucking, and loss of control of their boats because of the speed of the water in the trough. By the time they got to the bottom of the trough, they all knew that they had no chance to overcome this power of the water with so little speed or power. So after ten minutes, the admiral ordered them out of the trough. This was very hard for the captains to accept, for these men did not have quit in their vocabulary. With much concern, they began to pull out of the trough. This was an easy thing to do, and after five minutes, all three subs were out of the trough and heading back toward the carrier.

Vice Admiral Kingston ordered the hydrofoil submarine chaser that had just arrived on the scene into the trough to test their speed and control against the currents of the trough. The hydrofoil submarine chasers were capable of speeds of seventy to seventy-five knots. He also ordered the Pegasus class hydrofoils to try after the submarine chasers. The Pegasus class hydrofoil could reach speeds of just under one hundred miles per hour. After all of these tries and failures, Admiral Kingston was beside himself.

Meanwhile on the US *Nimitz*, the head of naval operations, Admiral Norstrum, started to speak to the men at roll call. "Gentleman, it is with the greatest concern that I am speaking to you. We have tried repeatedly with our nuclear subs to get into the trough on the outside of the storm but have not been able to stay in the trough. We are not fast enough, and we keep being thrown out of it. We have lost one sub that was sucked inside of the tornado and did not have enough power or speed to break through the power of the storm to get out. We have tried cruisers and cutters, and they don't have the speed to have control over the ships at that speed in the trough. They keep getting thrown out also. There doesn't seem to be any way to use a ship to get the laser into position. I think we better think of another way to get the job done. Thank you."

CHAPTER 6

Meanwhile at World News Today, Walter Frogheight reported, "Every TV and radio station in the world has been broadcasting nonstop for the past two days. There is nonstop TV coverage from around the world at every coastal village, town, and city. On the coast of California from San Diego to Ventura, their news helicopters and news teams are at every coastal city. There are news teams from all over United States swarming to California's coast. Every newspaper and magazine photographer and news writer is covering this story. Every TV station in Southern California hasn't had a regular televised program in the past two days.

"The news media has named this storm, 'The Storm from Hell.' There is a traffic jam in Southern California, the likes of which has never been seen before. There are millions of people leaving the LA, Ventura, Orange County, and San Diego areas to find higher ground just in case the storm hits their areas. The people from newspapers, magazines, and TV stations are coming to the southland of California. People have been coming in by car, truck, railroad, airplane, and bus. Everyone staying or coming in is flooding to the beaches. All police, fire, and rescue vehicles are in service and on the move constantly. News, police, rescue, and every available coast guard helicopters are in the air.

"The beaches are absolutely flooded with people. There are more people on the beaches than in the middle of the summer. Every group you can think of—save the whales, save the earth, save the water, conserve our beaches, and marine land oceanographers—are all at the beaches. Special interest groups from everywhere are checking out a phenomenon that has never happened on our beaches in all of recorded time. There are special interest groups talking about how they are going to save the seals. Other interest groups, like save the whales, are talking about twenty whales that have been beached and have died in the past two days on the western coast of the United States. There are surfing groups that have decided that no matter where the surf is, they're going surfing. The surf that is breaking is completely different than any surf in this area before. There are people with every interest known to mankind at the beaches where there is no water.

"The fishing piers are stretched out over dry sand where there use to be water. They look like great railroad trestles that used to cross great expanses that just stopped in mid-air and went no further. The stench at the beach is overwhelming, with all the dead fish and marine life baking in the hot sun for the past two days. It has caused this horrendous stench over the beach areas and into the Los Angeles basin. There are literally millions upon millions of birds that have flocked to the beach to feast on this gourmet of rotting fish. Birds are not the only animals that come to the beach. There are dogs, cats, mice and rats, coyotes, raccoons, possums, and every other kind of small animal that you can think of. We've seen them all here on the beaches, where the water used to be, feasting on mountains of rotting fish. There is seaweed and crab traps with lines and ropes twisted between their broken pieces and heaped-up mounds. There are old rusted fishing poles and lures, broken bottles, and discarded cans all through anchors and pieces of rope and wreckage of all kinds. It is unbelievable the things we have found where the water used to be.

"We have found things that people have thrown away. Who expected to see all this trash at the bottom of our beautiful bays and jetties and harbors, serene beauty just out of sight of our eyes? At the bottom of a pristine cliff, a car almost unrecognizable was rusted and the wreckage almost gone.

"We have spent the day at the Long Beach harbor, where it is as busy as an anthill. People have decided to use this opportunity to shore up old piers and make repairs on ships and clean out rusted and damaged piers and docks. There are hundreds of trucks loaded with big and small rocks filling in cracks and crevices in places they could never get to before. Engineers from the city all over the harbor are checking broken lines or inspecting docks and buildings from a whole new perspective, things you can't see from under the sea or where the sea is no more. People are finding new treasures where the seas used to be. There are fishing boats that have found their way into the harbor just to find no way possible to unload their catch. Some fishing boats have fifty or sixty people pushing wheelbarrows filled with fish across long expanses of sand to the fish markets. It is hard to believe all of the changes that are taking place, all the hardships and miseries that have been caused by the storm called 'The Storm from Hell.' There are aquariums up and down the coast of California, Oregon, Washington, and Alaska that are in deep trouble because they depend on fresh salt water to keep their sea life alive.

"There is construction going on all around these aquariums, putting in pipes and pumps so that they can get to some fresh salt water to keep their precious sea life from perishing. Almost all shipping life has ceased. Most of the major activity on the water inside the harbor is from emergency vessels. There are a few small boats that were not caught by the receding water that are either in the harbor or that have gone out to sea with no way to get back to their slip to moor their boat.

"The big power plants like Edison, along the coast of California, that depend on water to cool their plants as they make electricity have been shut down. In San Onofre, between Los Angeles and San Diego, there is a big nuclear power plant that has been shut down also. Half of the electrical power to Los Angeles and Southern California has been temporarily lost.

"There are also big Hyperion plants up and down the western coast of the United States that use salt water to clean human refuse. They are all shut down.

"Except for the 10 percent of the sport fishing boats in California that were out on a long trip when the water receded, the sport fishing industry has completely died. There is no sport fishing industry right now and probably will not be for a good long time. If we took into consideration just the sport fishing business of the world and everything that's connected to it, the loss of revenues or monies would have to be in the tens of billions of dollars per day. So using this as an analogy, sport fishing being just 5 percent of the business that depends on the oceans of the world to supply their needs in the harbors of great and small cities all over the world, the loss of dollars and cents could be in the trillions of dollars per day. There are many other industries that have been devastated by these turns of event in our great oceans, such as cruise ships and water taxis, shuttling people back and forth to islands offshore, just to name a few. This is then the most devastating report that I have ever personally witnessed. My name is Walter Frogheight reporting to you from World News Today at station WBS. This report was made possible with help from the National Geographic Foundation and the United States Coast Guard Weather watch in cooperation with the United States government."

While Jerry and Lydia had been busy for the past two hours, Tom had a break and was able to listen to the entire broadcast. This program really hyped Tom up. He just had to talk to someone and tell them what was going on. Tom wanted to tell Jerry all about it, but Jerry was busy with all the brass in a conference and couldn't be disturbed. Lydia was with her dad doing business with NASA weather. Tom looked around the base and found Gunner out on the runway watching the mechanics working on his Coast Guard Hurricane Watch aircraft. Tom approached Gunner excitedly and couldn't wait to tell him all the things that were going on around the world at all the beach cities and resorts. Gunner listened intently as Tom rattled on for at least forty-five minutes on all the things that were going on. Gunner expressed to Tom that his hopes and prayers were that this storm could be tamed in a very short period of time, because it seemed to him that it would take a long time for the coastal communities of the world to recover from such a devastating blow. Gunner was a man who didn't have much to say, with a heart as big as the universe. He would do anything to help anyone at any time. *This man really cares about people,* Tom thought to himself as he told Gunner that he had to return to the conference. As Tom turned to return to the conference, he waved a friendly good-bye to Gunner and then departed.

At the conference, Jerry had been terribly busy all of the afternoon and into the evening. Jerry had been dealt some devastating blows with the failure of the submarines because of the power of the storms. After trying many different kinds of ships and failing all along the journey, there was a slow down. What a relief! It was a well-needed break from things. But before he could get a break, he was involved with some heavy conversation with Admiral Hunly.

"How about an off-shore racer?" Jerry asked. "Can they reach speeds of over one hundred and fifty miles per hour?"

"I think that's a little risky," replied Hunly. "I mean, isn't it too small for the job?"

"No, not at all. The boats only have to carry the laser to guide the missiles to their destination," said Jerry.

"We do have an eighty-five-foot combat off-shore racer with a four-man crew and gun turret that is computerized that can reach those speeds and better. I guess they can be fitted to carry the laser," said Hunly.

Just then, the *Challenger* interrupted on the radio, "Houston, this is the *Challenger*. We are approaching the storm for our second pass. We are over the Pacific between California and the storm, and it looks like the entire Pacific fleet is out here. We have a fix on the storm and will send information back to you as fast as it comes in. It looks like our monster is getting bigger by the hour. Our readings are telling us that the water level in the tornado is about two thousand feet above sea level. We have spectrum readings on the ozone layer, and it is still growing. The bulge is fifteen miles high now and looks like a big bubble."

"Is there anything else we can do from here?" asked Houston.

"Not at this time," *Challenger* replied. "We will just keep sending your data and pray."

Jerry looked around and found Larry and asked him if he knew anything about cleaning up oil spills. Larry had a puzzled look on his face.

Larry replied, "Well, yes, but why do you ask?"

Jerry said, "I would like to know if there is a way that you can make crude oil more elastic."

"The three reps from the shell oil company are at the air force base because the supertanker *Hong Kong Queen* is full of Shell's crude oil," said Larry.

Larry looked across the room and called to a man in blue jeans to come over and then introduced him to Jerry. "Jerry, this is Todd McFadden. He is head of research for Shell Oil Company. I think he just might be able to answer some of your questions."

Jerry asked, "Todd is there any way to make crude oil more elastic?"

Todd said, "Yes there is. Why do you ask?"

Jerry expounded, "Would it be possible to take a large quantity of crude oil and mix it with something and then spread it against the ice to make something like a rubber covering so that the ice would not break?"

Todd spoke. "I suppose that if you first take sodium nitrate and mixed it with vinegar and with a very little boric acid. Then, mix it with the crude oil. Then last you could spread it over the salt water. When it hits the ice, it would have a chemical reaction that would make it like a rubber coating."

Jerry asked, "Is there any way you could make some of it sink?"

Todd answered, "Yes, if you put a salt solution between the oil and the ice."

Jerry asked, "Is the salt in the sea enough to do the trick?"

Todd answered, "I think so, but if not, we can just add some salt."

Jerry questioned Todd, "Could we do this on a giant scale like two million gallons in a supertanker in the middle of that storm? If I give you all the data about the storm and the tanker, could you come up with all the data I need in less than an hour?"

Todd excitedly replied, "I will get right on it."

Admiral Hunly walked up and stopped Jerry and replied to his earlier question. "Yes, Jerry, we have the boats on their way. The lasers will be installed on site from the aircraft carriers USS *Nebbits*, *Saratoga*, and *Constitution* in the designated coordinates you have requested. We will be operational in ninety minutes."

Jerry replied to the admiral, "We will need the sub to rendezvous with the supertanker in the middle of the storm."

Admiral Hunly replied, "Yes, we have been in contact with Captain Spencer aboard the *Alabama*, and he is in contact with Captain Farington on the super tanker."

Admiral Hunly looked at Jerry sternly and said, "Now these boats that we hope will do the job for us are experimental class and top secret. What I tell you goes no further. Okay?"

Jerry replied, "Okay, you've got my word on it."

Admiral Hunly started his briefing with Jerry. He called the offshore racers Fast Attack Hydrofoil Missile Launchers Experimental or FAHMLX. These boats were eight-five feet long and twenty-eight feet wide, with a draft of only three feet. They have four twelve-cylinder engines with over 30,000 horse power. They reach speeds of over 165 miles per hour comfortably. They are of high strength composite construction, and the displacement is only twenty-two tons. They have navigation radar, fire-control radar system, and are all integrated with surface-search radar. They have infrared seeker control and radar-seeker control and carry four MIM-72C Sea Chaparral ship-launched missiles infrared seeker control and two Rim-7H Sea Sparrows ship-launched point-defense surface-to-air missiles with radar seeker control that reach speeds of over mach four, which is over twenty-four hundred mph. These boats are like scorpions on the water.

These boats have a crew of four with a thirty mm gun turret with a computer control system that could be replaced with the laser and guidance system in a matter of minutes. These boats had everything that you could think of at a cost of twenty five million apiece, and nothing was left out! The boats could even be run by remote control from satellite, ship, or from an airplane. Jerry could see that Admiral Hunly was very proud of these boats.

Just then Jerry got a call from Todd McFadden about the crude oil.

Jerry said to Admiral Hunly, "I will be right back with you in five minutes.

"Todd, talk to me and tell me what we can do," said Jerry.

Todd replied, "I have all of the data for the chemicals and the amounts and the coordinates. I have given them to Colonel Thompson. He assures me that he would have all of the chemicals in the amounts loaded on the appropriate air transport planes and immediately ready to be in place in the next five hours. By my calculations, the oil should be dumped from the tanker starting in one hour and twenty minutes. By the time the oil reaches the wall of the storm, all of the chemicals will have time to mix properly and we should have the biggest balloon ever made in all of time."

"Thanks, Todd," said Jerry. "I could never thank you enough. Let's hope this works. Talk to you later."

Jerry went back and told Admiral Hunly all that had happened. He let Admiral Hunly know that he had to make arrangements to tell the captain and owners of the super tanker that they must release all of their cargo now and make arrangements to pick up the captain and his crew from the super tanker.

Meanwhile, the first US coast guard helicopter arrived on the scene at the iceberg and found it was in for the shock of its life. They found over seventy people in this small village 140 sled dogs. One woman was having a baby and needed medical attention. Luckily there was a doctor and nurse on the second helicopter that landed five minutes later. People had been packing their belongings for the last few hours, and there were hundreds of boxes and hundreds of suitcases filled with their belongings. There were ten helicopters in all and one cargo type ski plane. There was no problem loading all the people in the helicopters and flying them out, and there was also no problem loading the cargo plane with all the boxes and suitcases. The only problem was the 140 dogs. How do you move one hundred and forty dogs? So the solution was to call for another cargo plane and bring 140 dog cages to keep the dogs in while they transported them to the mainland.

Nine helicopters flew to the mainland with all but a few people. The second helicopter with the doctor, nurse, and pregnant woman and her husband and two children went directly to the aircraft carrier hospital. When they landed on the aircraft carrier, two nurses pushed a gurney, and the ship doctor met them. They took the woman and the child out of the helicopter and placed them on the gurney. They rushed the woman and her family below to the hospital.

Meanwhile, two thousand miles north of the storm, the icebergs that Gunner had found were still moving southward with the coast guard cutter following and exploring as it traveled around the west end of this gigantic iceberg. There were a lot of other ships in the area and enough planes and helicopters to start a small air force between the icebergs and the storm.

One of the helicopters flying from the iceberg to the storm found something very unusual about midpoint. They decided to investigate. What they found was that the river that was moving very fast, just like the water moves in the Grand Canyon, churning and bubbling. And it seemed to be moving too fast. They charted its position and called the aircraft carrier and asked for a Hawkeye to come and give them assistance surveying the river at this point. A Hawkeye is a plane that has a funny-looking dish on top of it. It is a radar plane that is hooked up with the Navistar satellite system. When the Hawkeye got within fifty miles of the helicopter, they were able to start plotting and mapping the area with the help of the satellites. By the time the Hawkeye and the helicopters were within visual range, they were done with their mapping and plotting procedures. What they found was a shallow water reef that was north to south about ten miles wide and east to west approximately ninety miles long. The water level was ninety feet deep, and the river was running directly over the center of the reef.

When the report was sent out, it not only went to the aircraft carriers but also directly to Edwards Air Force Base, where Tom had been watching all of the reports coming in from Storm Safe.

It was about 1:00 a.m. when Tom finally spotted the report, and it clicked in his head like a flash of lightning. He thought back to the flight from Long Beach to Edwards Air Force Base and his conversation with Jerry. *Jerry said that first we had to drain the water from the tornado and second we had to cut off the flow of cold water.*

Bingo! Tom thought. *I can't wait to find Jerry and tell him the good news.*

Tom found Lydia sleeping in a chair, and she looked very uncomfortable. As he looked up from Lydia, he saw Larry Walsh and walked up to him and said, "I think it's time we take a few hours break and catch a few Z's. I will see if I can find Jerry. Can you find Colonel Thompson to set up a break? I will be right back!"

Tom found Jerry and said to him, "Jerry, it's time for some sleep. Larry is setting it up with Colonel Thompson as we speak. Lydia is already sleeping in a chair, and she looks very uncomfortable."

In less than five minutes, Larry, Tom, Lydia, and Jerry were on their way to their quarters. On the way to their quarters, Tom filled Jerry in on the report about the shallow water reef. They were very tired by the time they got to their cabins. As soon as their head hit their pillows, they were all fast asleep.

It was 4:30 a.m., and the phone rang. It was Colonel Thompson giving them a wake-up call.

Jerry answered the phone, "Hello!"

On the other end of the phone the colonel. He explained to Jerry that the car would be there to pick them up in about thirty minutes.

"There are about a hundred new events that I need to fill you in on over breakfast," said the colonel. "I will see you in the mess hall. Good-bye."

Jerry woke Tom up as he was getting dressed.

Once Jerry was dressed, he walked next door to wake Lydia and her father. As he reached the door to their cabin, he heard some talking, so he listened quietly outside. He heard Larry and Lydia praying. Lydia spoke clearly, "Dear Lord, help Jerry to have the wisdom to face the battles ahead. Help us to be of help to him. And most of all, Lord, please be with us every step of the way and to help us see the answers to all of the complex questions and decisions we will face in the next few days. Lord, I believe you have sent Jerry to us to help us with this situation. Bless him, Lord, today. In Jesus' name we pray."

As Lydia was ending her prayer, Jerry made a noise as if he had just arrived. Larry then got up and answered the door and said, "Good morning, Jerry. We were just finishing our morning prayer. The colonel just called us, and I assume he called you also. We will be ready in five minutes."

Jerry answered, "Okay," and returned to finish a cup of coffee he started. Jerry thought to himself, *Gosh, not only is Lydia beautiful on the outside, but she is also so beautiful within. What a woman.*

Just then the car arrived, and Jerry met Lydia and Larry. They all got in the car and started toward the mess hall at the base.

On the way, Tom reviewed what he had told Jerry the night before. When they got to the mess hall, the colonel was waiting. Colonel Thompson filled them in over breakfast on all of the things that they had missed while asleep.

Meanwhile, at the hangar at Edwards Air Force Base, Gunner got his orders to go to the iceberg and went to see Colonel Thompson. Gunner found the colonel in the mess hall with Larry, Lydia, Jerry, and Tom. As Gunner walked up to the table where they all were eating, he said with a laugh in his voice, "I thought I would find you all here feeding your faces."

Gunner talked with the colonel for a few minutes about taking Tom with him on his assignment and as an adviser. Tom had this look on his face like a little child saying to his parents, "Please, please, can I? Can I? Please can I?" When the colonel said yes, you could see how relieved and happy Tom was. Gunner and Tom said their good-byes and walked out like they were two schoolboys about to play hooky as they laughed and skipped toward the hanger.

Colonel Thompson laughed and looked at Tom and Gunner as they went off to the hanger. "They're like a couple of kids!" he exclaimed. "But now we need to get serious about what is going on." Colonel Thompson's face got so serious Jerry wondered what was going to be said.

The colonel then proceeded, "The air force and navy seals have gathered together a force of twenty top demolition experts and supertanker builders to be placed on the deck of the supertanker with enough explosives to dump all of the crude oil of the tanker in a shorter time. The tanker has been dumping oil for the past four hours and only dumped one quarter of the cargo out. Now the rest has to be dumped in the next four hours. The captain has changed course and has gotten further from the center of the storm so that when the oil is dumped, it will take more time to reach the wall of the storm. They have thought about using a sub to torpedo the tanker, but the possibility of fire is too great and that had to be scrapped and another plan takes its place. Then came in two jet helicopters and landed on the deck of the tanker and the men went right to work to lay their explosives. This is very hard work because the explosives have to be placed below the waterline.

"The work was hard and tedious, but the air force and navy seals accomplished their task in about ten minutes. The whole operation took less than thirty minutes from start to finish. The helicopters picked up the demolition experts and tanker builders and the tanker crew with the captain and started back to the aircraft carrier USS *Nimitz*. As they left the tanker, they could see great quantities of crude oil leaving the tanker and knew that their mission had been successful. The submarine *Alabama* with Captain Spencer was standing by and waiting for the crude oil to be far enough from the tanker so that she can be sunk fast to the bottom. The tanker couldn't be allowed to cause trouble with the wall as they began to empty out this monster.

"They really didn't need any more troubles with this thing. When the tanker was five miles from the last traces of oil, Captain Spencer gave the orders to fire the torpedoes. They fired eight torpedoes from bow to stern. The ball of fire appeared huge. When the smoke cleared, they could see the tanker going down like a big rock. They followed it to the bottom with their sonar. They have never seen a ship go down so fast. The combination of torpedoes and demolition tore that tanker wide apart. This must be a record! The captain reported the tanker fell twelve thousand feet in less than five minutes."

"Now at this time, the skies were full of weather planes around the tornado and in the hurricanes collecting data for the big finale or the big disaster! And in the operations room at Edwards Air Force Base, the data was being processed as fast as possible. The countdown was at its fever pitch and the stage was set and the time was at hand. The reports said that the water level was two thousand and ninety feet above sea level and the storm wall speed was one hundred and twenty five miles per hour.

"At the storm, the boats had been fitted and were at the trough and ready. The oil had been dumped and the chemicals had been placed and mixed and salt has been laid at the inside of the wall.

"All things seem to be ready."

CHAPTER 7

At the operations room at Edwards Air Force Base, Lydia, Larry, and Jerry had just finished eating and returned to the operations room. They began to survey all of the data that had been collected. Jerry spotted something that was very alarming to him and began to check it out. The report from one of the weather planes outside of the tornado said that there was water spilling over the wall of the tornado, and it sent Jerry's mind in a whirlwind.

Jerry turned to Colonel Thompson, head of operations, and said, "Colonel, we need to have more information about the outside of the wall to see if there is water coming over the wall."

Colonel Thompson filled in Admiral Hunly and had that information back in a matter of minutes. "Yes, Jerry," said the colonel. "There is water spilling over the wall."

"Admiral," Jerry said, "this spells real trouble. If the water is spilling over the wall, this means that the wall is going to get thicker and we will find that the waters will get deeper within the tornado at an alarming rate. When the canopy of the earth moves out far enough, it will have to burst. At the rate that this thing is going, it looks as if we don't have a lot of time left!"

After hearing Gunner's report from the iceberg and the report of the shallow water reef two hundred miles ahead of the iceberg, Jerry called Admiral John L. Norstrum, commander of operations aboard the USS *Honolulu*.

"Admiral Norstrum, this is Jerry Turner."

Jerry began by briefing Admiral Norstrum at first about the shallow water reef ahead of the iceberg and then explained that the iceberg would be going over the shallow water reef in the next ten to twenty hours.

"Could we make the bottom of the icebergs like a wedge," asked Jerry, "so that it will move up over the shallow water reef and jam it so that it cannot move or go around the shallow water reef? Can we do this and plan it to act as a barrier to change the course of the river?"

The admiral broke in, "Well, I don't know. We have never tried something like this before. It is liable to break the icebergs up into smaller pieces."

Jerry replied, "We don't want to do that if we can find a way to jam that iceberg on the shallow water reef at the right time. Then this will be the final blow to the storm. You see, this icy river is the fuel that is supplying the tornado, and if we can shut off the fuel, then the storm will not be able to start all over again."

By this time Admiral Norstrum had already given orders to head for the iceberg.

Admiral Hunly ordered a full complement of two destroyers, three subs and one sub chaser, six helicopters, and two airplanes with two Hawkeyes to the iceberg. Six helicopters had already been loaded and sent from the mainland. Each helicopter had four sound teams aboard for checking the thickness of the ice. The helicopters left about the same time Gunner and Tom left for the iceberg. When the first helicopter arrived at the leading edge of the iceberg, they began by setting up teams every four miles. As all the helicopters and other teams got in place, they started sounding.

The sounding teams and the Hawkeye in the sky combined with the Navistar system moved the team away from the leading edge of the icebergs at five mile intervals. They were able to map the iceberg in a three-dimensional pattern. This information was being fed to the aircraft carriers, and the engineers aboard the aircraft carrier were able to determine that there were three bad spots on the bottom. One of the bad spots was twenty-two miles from the leading edge of the iceberg. The other two bad spots were sixty miles from the leading edge of the iceberg. While they analyzed this information, the engineers on the aircraft carrier found the best way to fix the problem. There were three submarines sent to the iceberg.

They positioned the submarines and got ready. The engineers told the submarines to coordinate the depth to fire her torpedoes. The first submarine fired two torpedoes. It was a perfect hit, and there were pieces of ice all over the place under the iceberg. The helicopters sat down a pattern of twenty-five miles of sounders, and they sent the information to the carrier. The reply from the carrier was that this was a huge success. Now they only had two more to go. After repeating this two more times, everything was a big go. This definitely was working,

Earlier, Admiral Hunly had ordered the aircraft carrier USS *Nimitz* to station itself at the west end of the iceberg. The admiral also ordered the aircraft carrier USS *Ranger* to station itself at the east end of the iceberg.

The winds from the hurricanes had stirred up big swells and finally reached the iceberg's positions. These swells were twenty to thirty feet high. These high swells were beginning to make maneuvering a little more difficult. The water around the iceberg had been filling with ships in the last two hours. The aircraft carriers were directing traffic in the area of the iceberg. There were at least six hundred naval ships in the area of the iceberg and over five hundred civilian ships. It looked like every ship that could leave its harbor was out at sea.

"The attack boats are ready," replied Admiral Hunly. "To make things easier, we will call them X1, X2, and X3. Captain Jack Sommers commands the X1, Captain Peter Porter the X2, and Captain Frank Jones the X3.

Admiral David Hunly then proceeded to order the captains to bring the boats in to the trough. "Captain of the X1, proceed to take the boat into the trough."

He ordered the other captains to do the same. As they entered the trough at a speed of one hundred miles per hour, they found that their speed was too slow and they didn't have much control over their boats. Captain Jack Sommers ordered their speed to exceed the speed of the trough, which was over 130 miles per hour.

When the boats reached 150 miles per hour, reports came from Porter and Jones that they now had very good control in the trough. They were now heading for the bottom of the trough. Captain Jack of the X1 reported to Admiral Hunly. "Admiral Sir, we have no problems and have full control of our boats should be in position in five to seven minutes. Over."

Back at Edwards Air Force Base, Jerry said to Admiral Hunly, "Sounds like we're ready to go. Is everything in place? Are the planes ready?"

Admiral Hunly replied, "All is ready, Jerry."

"According to our data, we need to proceed immediately," said Jerry.

The admiral replied "May God be with us."

Captain Jack of X1 said to Admiral Hunly, "Sir, we're in position. Do you want us to proceed?"

Admiral Hunly replied, "Let Operation Storm Safe begin."

Captain Jack of the X1 began to order Captain Porter and Jones, "Count down five, four, three, two, one. Begin."

The boats began to fire the lasers at the right coordination on the face of the wall. When they all had the lasers fixed in the right position, the signal was then given to the airplanes, and the first missiles were fired.

The first missiles hit, and there was a gigantic explosion. Chunks of ice the size of houses had fallen down the wall and splashed in the water just hundreds of feet from the boats that were going 150 miles per hour. Some chunks had fallen over the boat smaller in size, and other chunks of ice as big as footballs were hitting the boat.

"Let's hope one of the house-size chunks of ice doesn't hit one of the boats," replied Captain Jack. He then added, "There's a hole in the ice that we can see that you can put three or four football fields in. It seems to be gigantic."

As the second set of missiles hit inside of the first hole, more chunks of ice began to fly out of the hole, some streaming down, some flying out. The captains of the boats were now changing courses to miss being hit by the big chunks of ice. The crew was scurrying and doing the things they needed to do, keeping their eyes open for any danger as the missiles hit deep inside the hole. The hole was enlarging, and gigantic chunks were falling down the wall of the hole. As the fifth and sixth of these missiles came in, big chunks of ice were no longer a danger to the boats because it took them time to come down the hole. They were now falling down the hole covered in water, and it was easier to keep the boats under control and the lasers fixed deep inside the holes created by the missiles as they continued to fly into the hole and explode.

The first wave of airplanes had left and gone back to the carriers, and now the second wave had already released their missiles. The hole was one mile deep now. It seemed to be approximately one to two miles in diameter. The second barrage of missiles from the second wave of airplanes was complete. They had left to return to the carrier. The third wave of planes had just fired their missiles, and the missiles were tracking the laser into the hole perfectly.

"There is an awful lot of ice debris coming out of the hole," replied Captain Jack.

Every once in awhile, one of the missiles hit the debris and exploded, and it seemed that they would have to use more missiles than they had thought.

The third wave of planes had finished firing their missiles and left for the carrier, and now the forth had begun to fire their missiles. The data from the laser showed that they were now two miles deep into the wall as explosion after explosion appeared in the hole. Missile after missile flew up the hole. The fourth wave was now over, and the fifth began.

They were now at the twelfth wave of airplanes, and water flow increased out of the hole. The laser depth read five miles deep. Hopefully, they'd be breaking through the wall shortly, as the thirteenth wave of airplanes began to fire their missiles. As their third missile fired, the hole that was two miles in diameter began to fill with water. In fact, it started to pour out so hard that the positioning of the boats had to be moved away from the hole.

Water came out so fast that it moved the entire ten to twelve miles to the bottom of the trough and was becoming an endangerment to the boat. Captain Jack ordered the other two boats to move away from the bottom of the trough. They proceed as ordered. For the next five minutes, water continued to flow out of the holes. But then hole number two from ship X2 reported to Captain Jack that the water flowing from hole number two had ceased. Captain Jack ordered Peter Porter back to the bottom of the trough with the laser fixed. The planes were ordered to fire into hole two, with two missiles fired. The hole began to open up, and the water began to flow again,

A report from the submarine inside the tornado came to Admiral Hunly. The depth of the water on the inside of the tornado had only raised six feet in the past half hour.

Back at the base, Jerry spoke to Admiral Hunly. "At this rate, sir, it will take too long to get rid of the water inside the tornado. The holes in the tornado wall will have to increase to ten miles in diameter."

Admiral Hunly ordered Captain Sommers and the other two boats as close as they could get to the bottom of the trough.

He ordered them to fix their lasers on a new hole in front of the first. Six miles in front of it, they began firing the missiles to start the new hole, knowing that when the holes grew, there would be much greater danger. Afterward, twelve more waves of airplanes and missiles shot into the second hole with a lot of evasive maneuvering of the boat.

The second hole was beginning to flow water. Captain Jack ordered the lasers moved to the center of the two holes and up two miles. Captain Jack ordered the next waves of the airplanes to attack the hole with the missiles all over again. Now, this was becoming a very dangerous situation. The holes were now spewing out water and chunks of ice as big as houses. The boats were now in a very dangerous position and trying to hold a position that could continue to track the lasers deep within the holes to finish knocking out the final wall. All of a sudden, a chunk of ice as big as the coliseum in downtown LA came out of hole number two and destroyed X2. All the crew was destroyed.

Admiral Hunly proceeded to order the X4 with Captain Mikael R. Taez into the trough with a final barrage of missiles. Simultaneously, the center of all three holes started to collapse and break free. Seeing this, Captain Taez warned the other captains of the impending danger and turned his boat hard right rudder and increased his speed. The other captains of X1 and the X3 followed his lead. As the captain of the X4 anticipated, the center of the three holes collapsed. There was a rumble as a chunk of ice, five miles wide and six or seven miles long, started sliding out of the hole. It crackled and crunched and scraped and slid. As one mile of ice was sticking out of the hole, the water pressure was so great that it broke and snapped like a lightning bolt. Water was thrown in the air hundreds of feet while it slid into the trough. The sliding of the next chunk continued its crackling, crunching, and scraping, as it also couldn't stand the pressure from the water it had entered and it broke off, snapping like a lightning bolt. It continued again following the same pattern as before about a mile, sticking out in the water.

The pressure of the water was building until it couldn't take it any longer. Then it snapped like a lightning bolt and started all over again. Only this time, the piece that came out was about two miles long, and it came thundering out rolling and bouncing.

"What a sight to see!" one of the captains said.

Tremendous amounts of spray from the iceberg came out of the hole and danced and splashed like a great whale. All three captains witnessed this at the same time, and all three were about three miles from the bottom of the trough. Just then, Captain Jack Sommers of the X1 told the other captains to head directly out of the trough at full speed. As the other captains turned their boats to go directly out of the trough and put the pedal to the metal, they could see a gigantic wave of water filling and coming out of this ten-mile diameter hole. The majestic wave seemed to move in slow motion as it came out and lay in the trough. It came down the wall side of the trough and filled it, and it began to climb the other side. As the water was filling the trough and coming closer to the boats, it seemed to go from slow motion to super speed and was moving much faster than the boats. When the boats were coming over the crest of the trough at the outside edge, they became airborne and seem to fly for hundreds of feet.

These boats moved at full speed and were being pushed by the centrifugal force of the trough. They must have been moving at better than two hundred miles per hour as they hit the water outside the trough.

One of the crew looked at Captain Summers and remarked, "Can you believe that? What a rush."

The boats must have been at least one mile from the edge of the trough as the water began to spill over. It had slowed considerably, and the boats were in no danger, as the trough was taking up almost all of the water from the holes. The captains turned their boats to position themselves in front of the hole just to find that time had run out on them and they were coming to the hurricane. They broke away from the trough and started heading for the hurricane behind them.

It took them over an hour to get back to where they began at the hurricane behind them. As they reached the edge of the hurricane, the hole appeared from behind the hurricane. They found the hole in the ice much bigger than it was earlier when they had left. Water flowed out perfectly.

The water level inside of the tornado was falling. The water had fallen 130 feet. At this rate, it would take four days to empty out the tornado, so it was decided to wait two hours and start all over again. This way, there would be six holes in the wall. This would release 260 feet of water every four hours in half the time. X1, X3, and X4 entered the trough again to use their lasers. They guided the missiles to their destination to open three new holes. Four hours later, with their job complete, three new holes were opened and everything was going smooth. Captain Sommers ordered the boats out of the trough. The seas were getting bigger now, and there were forty-foot swells. This slowed the boats down as they turned to go back toward the hurricane that they had left four hours before.

After about thirty minutes, Captain Sommers ordered the boats back into the trough where the water conditions were better. After one and a half hours, they came to one of the holes. Captain Sommers ordered the boats out of the trough to go around the hole. After passing the hole, Captain Sommers ordered the boats back into the trough again. As they passed the hole, they could see that the hole was getting bigger and the water was flowing very well with no problems. After they got to the hurricane, Captain Sommers ordered the boats to stand by and hold their position in case there were any further problems. As the X5, X6, and X7 came into position to take their places, Captain Sommers ordered X1, X3, and X4 to leave their positions. After leaving their positions, they were to meet up with a refueling tanker to refuel at sea. After refueling, they were to return to their positions and stand by.

CHAPTER 8

Back at Edwards Air Force Base, Jerry had been looking very hard at the iceberg and the distance between it and the shallow water reef. Taking a calculator and figuring the distance between the icebergs and the shallow water reef, Jerry found that the icebergs would be at the shallow water reef ten hours ahead of schedule.

Jerry thought to himself, *This can't be. If we shut off the water to the tornado before it is emptied out, the integrity of the wall will be compromised. This could cause the wall to collapse. If this happens, then all we have done will be for nothing. We will still have a tidal wave, and everything will be lost.*

Jerry was in a real quandary. His thoughts were racing a hundred miles a minute in every direction. Jerry thought to himself again, *Here it goes again—the butterflies in the stomach, the headache, the anticipation, and the sick feelings and distress. All the signs are there.*

As he tried to clear his thoughts, Lydia walked up to Jerry and spoke to him very softly, "A penny for your thoughts!"

Jerry turned his head slightly and looked into Lydia's eyes and said, "My thoughts are not worth a penny right now."

Lydia smiled slightly and said, "No they're not worth a penny, they are worth thousands of dollars."

Lydia detected that Jerry was pondering a very difficult decision. She could see that Jerry was going through great pain and really needed help. Now if there was anything that Lydia was capable of, that would be discerning when someone really needed to be lifted up. So Lydia said with a smile on her face, "Cheer up! Things could get worse, and they already have for the past five days. You have risen to the occasion so many times that I know you already have the answer and there's really nothing for anyone to worry about, Jerry. Give me one of those great big handsome smiles of yours and let's talk about it."

Jerry couldn't help himself. He burst out with laughter and a smile. Jerry said, "Lydia," after laughing for over a minute.

"You know the moment you made me laugh, the revelation of what has to be done hit me like a ton of bricks. It seems like every time I'm at a crisis, you show up and seem to know exactly what to say to lift my spirit up. It's like you have a sixth sense and know my very thoughts. You really are a godsend." Jerry sighed.

Lydia blushed and replied to Jerry, "I don't know what it is, but it seems like when you're really worried about something. I either see it on your face or I feel it inside of me. Now that should reassure you that everything is okay. So what is it that's bothering you?"

Jerry said, "It's that stupid iceberg. It is going to arrive at the shallow water reef ten hours before it should. But the revelation is all we have to do is slow that iceberg down to buy us the time that we need to empty out the tornado. So you see, you pulled me out of another one."

Lydia said with a slight chuckle, "Oh, is that all? I thought you had a real problem."

Lydia kissed Jerry on the cheek and turned and walked away. Jerry thought to himself, *It's as if she knew just what I needed then came to me and gave it to me. Now that she has given me what I need, it is back to work and business as usual.* He left his thoughts behind.

Jerry then proceeded to call Vice Admiral Edwin R. Kingston of the US Pacific Fleet Carrier Groups One and Seven, Naval Air Force Commander.

"Hello. Is this Vice Admiral Kingston?" Jerry asked.

"Yes," the admiral replied.

"This is Jerry Turner. I have a problem."

Admiral Kingston said to Jerry, "Son, it is such a pleasure to finally meet you, even if it is over the phone. And please call me Ed. Let's talk about the problem and see if there's anything I can do to help."

Jerry replied, "Thank you, Sir, I mean Ed. You know, this has really put me at ease. I was very nervous when I realized I would be talking to such an important man in the navy. I have been checking the data to use the icebergs to change the flow of the ice river. As you know, there is a shallow water reef approximately one hundred and fifty miles ahead of the iceberg. If the iceberg reaches this shallow water reef too soon, it will starve the wall of the tornado, and it may destroy the integrity of the wall. You see, the storm should be empty before we shut off the flow of the river, because the river ensures the integrity of the wall. With all the reports I have here at Edwards Air Force Base, it seems to me that there may be enough ships in the area of the iceberg that we could use the ships to slow down the iceberg.

The admiral replied to Jerry, "Great idea! This is just down my alley. How much time do you need to buy?"

Jerry replied, "It looks to me like the tornado will be drained in twenty hours but the icebergs will be at the shallow water reef in about ten hours. If we could buy ten hours or slow the iceberg down from twenty knots to ten knots, then I think we will be able to finish the tornado off."

The admiral replied to Jerry, "You've got it, son. Consider the ships to gather at the iceberg within the hour. You have my word on that."

"Thank you, sir," said Jerry.

"Drop the sir and call me Ed," replied the admiral.

"Thank you, Ed," Jerry hesitantly said.

"No, thank you!" Admiral Kingston replied. "It is a pleasure to work with someone who knows exactly what they are doing. It is my pleasure to be of help."

When Jerry got off of the phone, he felt like a king. The admiral had really put his mind at ease.

Admiral Kingston immediately set up a conference with all naval captains to get preparations under way for what he called, "Iceberg Push."

Back at Edwards Air Force Base, Lydia was watching a news clip.

"Good evening. This is Connie Pong reporting to you from Channel 3 News in Los Angeles. This evening's top story is about over four million people coming to the Mile High City, Denver, Colorado.

Our story tonight starts with the floods of people coming from California, Oregon, Washington, and many other states that border the oceans. When a large number of people enter a city, it can cause many problems for the city and all its governmental agencies. When four million people invade a city, the flood of problems becomes too gigantic to even comprehend.

"The first problem is you have to have enough food and water for a city that has a capacity of six million people. When you add four million more, you have a burden to that city that they may not be able to cover. The army, marines, and national guard have been sitting up tent cities all over the suburbs of Denver for the past two days. All of the grocery stores are very low on food and bottled water. Trucks are moving to and from the grocery stores on double shifts. There is now a shortage of gasoline at the service stations. Fuel prices have doubled in the past day and are expected to double again tomorrow. People's tempers are short, and their pocketbooks are getting shorter.

"Every city and government agency is working overtime trying to keep a handle on the expanded population. The armed forces and the national guard are keeping a pretty good handle on this double population. There have been reports of looting, and robbery is on the rise. The national guard is on top of this problem. Very little of it has gotten by unseen. All the parks in the surrounding areas of Denver are full to capacity, and Rangers are working double shifts. The jails here in Denver are full to capacity and bulging out at the seams. Every cell that holds one person is now holding four. The overcrowding is horrendous, and the food shortages are just as bad.

"Everyone is complaining that they can't get any help from any governmental agency. Although there are a hundred and twenty food kitchens that are run by the army, marines, and the national guard, all of the reports from the armed forces about food shortages say that everyone that comes gets fed without exception. Colonel Harington of the national guard stated to me that no one will starve.

"In the national news today, there has been a run on banks, with everyone in coastal cities closing their bank accounts and moving inland. Bank presidents have agreed that at this rate, the banks will be closed by tomorrow at the latest. They have further stated that if it had not been for the Federal Reserve Banks, they would have run out of money yesterday. Bankers are warning people that they are making themselves an easy target for robbers and hoods. To this very day, there have been reports of over four hundred people being killed in front of banks and ATM machines.

"There have been seventy-three armed robberies. Robbers have been shot and killed in the act of robbing someone in front of a bank or ATM machine. There have been another one hundred and eighty robbers under arrest throughout the United States. There have been more robberies and looting throughout the United States in the last two days than usual. It has been escalating, but a warning is going out through the news media that under martial law you can be shot on sight. It has been reported from the armed forces that over six hundred burglars, looters, robbers, and murderers have been shot in the act. It has been further stated by the armed forces that under martial law, we will not put up with this kind of conduct and the perpetrators will be dealt with on the spot.

"It has been reported in many major cities that there are cases of civil disobedience. But our armed forces seem to be 'Johnny on the spot' and put a stop to it with force if necessary with little or no resistance. Meanwhile, in local news, the surfers in California say they are in heaven. It seems that every beach you can find is a brand-new beach. With the water receding, there is not one beach that surfers have ever surfed before. So this makes it a surfer's paradise. It is a brand-new break. To make things even better, the surf on the West Coast of the United States, because of the storms, has grown to twenty feet. This, I have been told, is a surfer's paradise. Without exception, every surfer that hasn't left the coast is out surfing every day. This is Connie Pong, Channel Three, Los Angeles."

As Lydia channel surfed through different news broadcasts and newspapers, she picked up an article written by Jerry Robinson of the *Orange County Regal*, The article read, "Aye, Aye Sir! Fill 'er Up." In a tricky but routine maneuver at sea, US ships refueled off Southern California. All Lydia could think of was all the ships at sea, at this moment, fighting a monster that could very well destroy all of mankind and the Earth.

Lydia left the news program behind to go find Jerry. Just thinking about all of these problems that were caused by the storms in the Pacific had troubled Lydia, and she felt Jerry just might be able to help her feel better. *Just knowing that something is being done does help some,* she thought to herself. Lydia found Jerry and tapped him on the shoulder. When Jerry turned around and saw Lydia, he looked into her eyes and could see something was troubling her. Jerry said, "What's wrong?"

Lydia said, "Oh, you know, the storm and other things."

Jerry was heartbroken over the look in Lydia's eyes, knowing her tender heart couldn't take much of this gloom and doom. Jerry took a break and grabbed Lydia by the arm and began to walk toward the door of the conference room. As they were walking, Jerry spotted Colonel Thompson, and he and Lydia walked over to talk to the colonel. The colonel was busy but dropped what he was doing to talk to Jerry.

"Is there something I can get for you, Jerry?" asked the colonel.

Jerry replied, "How long would it take to get to the carrier that is next to the iceberg?"

The colonel had a puzzled look on his face and said, "About an hour."

Jerry asked the colonel if there was any way they could do their work from the carrier.

The colonel answered, "Well, that could be quite dangerous. After all, there are high seas and also the danger of a tidal wave."

Jerry said, "I don't think that will matter anyhow. If we have a tidal wave, we will also be hit here at Edwards Air Force Base. Lydia and I would like to carry on our business aboard the carrier."

The colonel said he would make the arrangements and he would get back with Jerry in five minutes or so. Jerry and Lydia turned and continued toward the door of the conference room and walked outside. It was a hot and sultry afternoon, and there wasn't very much shade outside the conference room.

Lydia turned to Jerry and said, "What are we doing going to the carrier?"

Jerry said, "Well, Lydia, this place is so full of gloom and doom. I thought it would be a welcome break. We will be able to see things firsthand from the carrier."

Lydia's face lit up as she replied, "That sounds like a great idea. I really need a break from this place. I feel like I need some sort of excitement or some sort of control over this situation with the storm and all."

Jerry and Lydia walked around for a few more minutes in the hot afternoon and then turned and walked back to the conference room. As they walked in the conference room, arm in arm, Colonel Thompson met them with a great big smile on his face.

Colonel Thompson remarked, "Have I ever got a surprise for you! There are two F14 Tomcat fighters waiting for you and the car is ready to take you to the hangar as we speak. These fighters have been refueled and are on their way back to the carrier now. They have orders to take you directly to the Aircraft Carrier USS *Ranger* stationed at the east end of the iceberg. Admiral John L. Nostrum, commander of operations aboard the US *Honolulu*, will meet you aboard the *Ranger* to help you with any of your needs. I am sure that you and Admiral Norstrum have talked many times already. This will be the perfect chance for you to meet Admiral Norstrum, Jerry."

Just then Lydia said to Colonel Thompson, "Can you tell my dad that I am going to the *Ranger* with Jerry?"

Colonel Thompson laughed. "I just told Mr. Walsh that you would be going too. Your dad told me that you were becoming a real jet setter nowadays, and we got a big laugh out of that. He told me to tell you that he sends his love with the two of you."

Just then Lydia turned and threw her arms around Jerry's neck. Bending her knees and picking her feet up in the air as she squeezed Jerry's neck, she remarked, "Thank you, Jerry! *Oh*, thank you! I really needed to get away."

After a moment, Lydia let Jerry go and turned back to the colonel and said with an embarrassing blush, "Thank you, Colonel. I really do need a break. There are so many horrible things going on that it is hard to bear some times."

Colonel Thompson walked Jerry and Lydia outside where the car was waiting, and as he helped them in to the car, he said, "If there is anything that you need, just ask. I guarantee it will be supplied, and don't forget to call me if you need anything."

The colonel closed the door of the car, and the driver headed for the runway. As they came to the runway, they could see two F14 Tomcat fighters sitting there.

Lydia turned and looked at Jerry and said, "Thank you, Jerry. You really do know what I need."

As they approached the planes, they could see two pilots with flight jackets and helmets to give to Jerry and Lydia. As they got out of the car, Jerry could see just how excited Lydia really was. Lydia grabbed Jerry by the hand and pulled him toward both planes excitedly as she skipped and bounced. When they got to the planes they were to board, Jerry introduced Lydia and himself to the pilots. The pilots introduced themselves also. Lydia's pilot was Lieutenant Bob Barnett, and Jerry's pilot was Lieutenant John Lance. Jerry and Lydia got their flight jackets on and carried their helmets as the pilots helped them into their seats. The pilots helped them put their helmets on as they instructed them on the things that were going to happen. They also instructed Jerry and Lydia how to communicate with the pilots and that they would help them with any off their needs. Jerry and Lydia had been on many commercial airplanes flying to different destinations in the past, but nothing could have prepared them for the experience they were about to encounter.

After the pilots started their planes and went through a checklist, they talked with the tower and got permission for takeoff. The pilots taxied the fighters and positioned themselves next to each other. They wanted to takeoff together side by side. The pilots hit the throttles, and those fighters began to move just like any commercial airplane. But after a few hundred feet, the pilots pushed the pedal to the metal, and Jerry and Lydia were pinned to their seats with about three G's of force, triple the sensation that you get when a commercial airplane takes off. As the planes left the runway, the pilots pulled the nose of their fighters almost straight up. Lydia and Jerry were having the ride of their life, a real thrill ride! In the middle of the climb to forty thousand feet, the pilots turned west and headed out to sea. Lydia and Jerry could see the Pacific Ocean already before they leveled off at forty thousand feet.

Lydia almost leaped from her seat and shrieked. "The thrill is so exciting." Her pilot, Bob, winked.

Then Lydia heard Jerry, over the radio, "You aren't kidding."

Lydia said, "I didn't know we could all talk to each other."

Jerry's pilot John said, "Sure, we're just one big happy family."

Pilot Bob spoke out and said, "This is usually a two-hour trip, but Colonel Thompson told us that you really wanted to get there in a hurry."

"Is that true?" Lydia smirked, "Does that mean you are really going to go fast?"

Just then the two pilots hit the throttle full. The same sensation that Lydia and Jerry had experienced on takeoff, they were able to experience again at forty thousand feet. In less than a minute, the sensation was gone, but they were still moving at almost Mach 2, which is almost fourteen hundred miles per hour.

Jerry screamed out, "What a rush! I have never felt anything like that before. You guys really got it made."

They were over the ocean in about fifteen to twenty minutes and about forty minutes from the carrier. As they looked out the cockpit window, they could see hundreds and hundreds of little white lines heading in the same direction as the iceberg. These lines were ships, and there were thousands of them.

Lydia thought to herself, "Gee! This storm hasn't slowed down shipping any."

The ride was smooth as they headed into the sun in the direction of the carrier.

Jerry spoke in the radio, "How are you doing over there, Lydia?"

Lydia sang, "Just fine. It is such a beautiful day, it just doesn't seem like all of this storm business can really be happening, although I know it really is."

Bob, Lydia's pilot, asked if she was comfortable and felt okay.

"I feel just fine," Lydia answered, and this is like an E-ticket at Disneyland."

Meanwhile, Vice Admiral Kingston had just finished a fleet-wide conference with all of his staff and ship captains. The conference was broadcast live, and Jerry and Lydia could hear it over the radio. In the conference, the admiral covered all the aspects of slowing down the iceberg for the next ten to twenty hours to give the tornado a chance to empty out before they shut off the icy river flow with the shallow water reef. They discussed traffic control by the carriers and the minimum size of ships that could participate.

"After all," said the admiral, "with twenty—to thirty-foot swells, smaller ships would have a hard time keeping their bow to the iceberg without tearing up their vessels."

They also discussed refueling at sea those ships that were low on fuel. Most of the navy ships that were called to action for Operation Storm Safe had been at sea for three days or better.

"Refueling has already started at the beginning of this operation and will continue," said the admiral. "Civilian shipping involved with the iceberg will be refueled at no cost to the ship captain or owner. There will be eight refueling tankers at all times. Four refueling tankers will be stationed at the east end of the iceberg, and the remaining four will be stationed at the west end of the iceberg. We have eighteen seagoing tags on site now, with twenty two more to be on sight within the hour. Any ship that has trouble will immediately be towed to the east or west end of the iceberg. All ships one hundred feet and larger can participate in slowing down the icebergs. All seagoing tugs can participate in slowing down the iceberg, with the exception of those nearest any ship in trouble. The nearest tug to a ship in trouble must break away from the icebergs and go to the aid of the ship that is in trouble. All civilian shipping will be under direct order of Admiral Norstrum aboard the aircraft carrier USS *Ranger*. There will be helicopters dropping small naval personnel parties to make sure that civilian shipping has the correct protocol and safety of the fleet involved. Any ship that does not comply with emergency regulations will be escorted out of the area immediately. This message has been sent to all naval and civilian shipping within a one-thousand-mile radius. This is Admiral Kingston, and I will report any updated information. Over."

"Wow! That was impressive," said Lydia.

Jerry spoke back to Lydia, "I had a long talk with Vice Admiral Kingston just before we left. That man doesn't mess around. He gets right after a problem. I am really impressed!"

As the pilots of the F-14s began to descend and slow down, Lydia and Jerry could see the iceberg.

Lydia yelled out, "Jerry, do you see that iceberg? It's as big as an entire state! There are so many ships out here. I never realized this iceberg was so big. All of these ships look like little toys next to that iceberg. How in the world are those ships going to slow down that iceberg? It's just so big."

Lieutenant John Lance broke in to the conversation at this point and told Jerry and Lydia that they would have to observe radio silence until they had landed on the aircraft carrier USS *Ranger*. Lieutenant John Lance contacted the carrier for landing instructions. Lieutenant Lance lined up to land first on the carrier deck. As the lieutenant brought the flaps down to slow the plane, Jerry felt like someone just hit the brakes. Jerry felt as if they were going to fall into the ocean before they reached the carrier's deck. He could see the flagman on the carrier deck now, and Lieutenant Lance was very busy keeping the plane under control. The wings seemed to be going up and down as the lieutenant maneuvered the plane skillfully to the deck of the carrier.

Jerry could hear the wheels hit the deck of the carrier, and at that exact moment, Jerry was pushed forward against his safety straps so hard that he thought his chest would break. Then the F-14 stopped dead in its tracks. For a moment, the fighter literally moved backward, and then Jerry could hear the sound of the engines of the fighter increase as they began to move forward. Another flagman guided them, about two hundred feet toward the main tower of the carrier. The cockpit was open now, and Jerry began to look around. In less than a minute, he heard the engines of the other F14 fighter pull up next to him on his right. As Jerry looked over at the other fighter, he could see Lieutenant Barnett and Lydia as the canopy was being raised. As Lieutenant John Lance shot down the engines on the F14, Jerry could see him taking off his helmet and getting out of the cockpit.

Lieutenant Lance then came back to where Jerry was seated and helped him with his safety belts and helped him take off his helmet. Lieutenant Lance could see an ear-to-ear smile on Jerry's face as he reached out to help him out of the plane. When Jerry was standing on the wing, he looked over and saw Lydia just stepping out of the other F14 fighter onto the wing. Lydia had the same ear-to-ear smile on her face as she waved to Jerry. As they both climbed down ladders to the deck of the carrier from the wing of the F14, they were escorted to the main tower of the aircraft carrier *Ranger*. They went through a door and down a corridor, where they entered a very large conference room. As they walked through the door, Admiral John L. Norstrum, commander of operations, met them.

Admiral Norstrum stretched out his hand to Jerry as he introduced himself and said, "You must be Jerry Turner. It is such a pleasure to finally meet you. And this must be Larry's beautiful daughter, Lydia." The admiral greeted her with a handshake also.

"Your dad told me you are an explorer and a jet setter these days." With a big smile on his face, the admiral explained to Lydia that he had just gotten off the phone with her dad. "We go back a long way. He and I have been friends for over thirty years, and I have seen pictures of you as you have grown up through the years."

CHAPTER 9

Admiral Norstrum escorted Jerry and Lydia to the center of the conference room where the command center was. Jerry noticed a big screen that hung from the ceiling to the floor. It wasn't like a TV screen because it was clear and you could see through it. In the middle of the screen was the iceberg, and all around the iceberg there were thousands of ships positioned. Admiral Norstrum began to show Jerry and Lydia that every ship had a position that they would be put in against the iceberg.

The admiral laughingly said, "We have a saying already, 'Bow to the 'Berg.' That's what all the sailors are saying. Put your bow to the 'berg and half speed ahead."

The admiral showed them the difference between the navy and the civilian ships, the navy ships being black and the civilian ships colored blue. The admiral showed them that if you looked closely, you would see each ship had been given a number and a letter. This was for the purpose of identification for each ship. You could tell from the command center if the ship was a civilian freighter or a naval destroyer.

"You see," said the admiral, "if I type in a certain number with a letter, the computer will bring up a picture of the ship. All the information on that ship will come up right here on the screen."

The admiral punched in a few numbers and a letter. Immediately on the screen in front of Jerry and Lydia, there was a picture of the USS *Ranger* and a full description of its complement of weapons, aircraft and the armament of the ship, where it was built, and all other pertinent information. Then the admiral typed in a different number and letter and a picture of a supertanker built in Iraq with the company that owns it, where it had come from, and its destination with the size and cargo.

Lydia said, "That's great! Can you do this with every ship out there?"

The admiral replied, "Well, almost every ship, but if we don't have a file on that ship we start one immediately."

The admiral cleared the screen and continued to explain how they had approximately four hundred of the smaller ships in the navy, like seagoing tugs, attack boats, and PT boats, were using submarines to escort the ships to their assigned places against the iceberg.

"We have to keep the ships far enough apart," said the admiral. "If they lose control and come up sideways against the iceberg, they will not hit another ship. We have already lost one ship. A freighter out of Peru lost her engine, and before we could get to her, she ended up sideways against the iceberg and was sucked under, with all hands aboard. There is absolutely nothing that we can do if we can't get to the ship quick enough to pull them to safety. You see, this iceberg weighs billions of tons, and we can only hope to slow it down. We really have no control over something the size of this iceberg. We have already escorted over two hundred and fifty ships into position, and in the next two hours, we should have over three thousand ships with their bows to the 'berg, so to say. It is really hard to believe that we are getting so much cooperation from so many different countries, sending their ships to battle this iceberg. If the reports of all the ships that will arrive in the vicinity of the iceberg in the next fifteen hours are true, we will have over twelve thousand ships wanting to help from over seventy different countries. We have engineers working feverishly to make sure the power that we use against the iceburg is not overloaded on one side or the other. If this were to happen, the iceberg could begin to turn, and that wouldn't be to our advantage. We are trying to keep the iceberg under control and keep it moving evenly."

Admiral Norstrum said, "Well enough of this for now. You might like to see your quarters and get cleaned up. Dinner will be served in the mess hall in about a half hour or so. Ensign Parker here will show you to your quarters. I will see you in the mess hall. We are having dinner at the captain's table."

Meanwhile, Tom and Gunner were flying around the iceberg when they received a call from an air tanker in position to refuel the coast guard rescue plane. Gunner turned the plane and began to climb to twenty thousand feet, where the refueling would take place.

Tom said to Gunner, "This will be a first for me."

Gunner replied to Tom, "Then you will really enjoy this."

All of a sudden, Tom spotted the refueling tanker. It was about a mile away and right in front of the coast guard plane. Tom could see the fuel arm coming out of the back of the refueling tanker. By the time Gunner got close enough to the tanker, the coast guard planes had slowed down to approximately two hundred miles per hour. As Gunner maneuvered the big coast guard plane into position, Tom thought to himself, *This really is hard. I hope I don't have to do this.*

It looked very tricky, and Tom believed that it should take a lot of skill and practice. Gunner eased the plane skillfully under the fueling arm and could hear and feel the arm connecting to the coast guard plane. Gunner reached over and flipped a couple of switches and then said with a sigh of relief, "This will take about ten minutes."

Gunner looked up at Tom and said, "On a long flight like this, we will have to refuel every twelve to fourteen hours."

"You really are good at this, Gunner," said Tom. "It must take a lot of practice."

"Tom, after doing this for years, it's really very easy. Just like riding a bike. After a while, you just don't think about it. It just happens," said Gunner.

Tom thought to himself, *For the past six or eight hours, Gunner and I have been flying around the iceberg and watching the ships put their "bows to the 'berg," as the sailors say. They had turned around when the freighter went down in front of the iceberg. We flew south to check on the shallow water reef. We heard the commotion over the radio and didn't find out until later that all hands went down with their ship.*

This was very sad for Gunner and the crew of the Coast Guard Hurricane Watch Airplane. Tom was thinking about it all as he was looking out of the window and saw all of the ships in front of the icebergs. Tom was moved, but he knew this would not be the only ship to go down in front of this iceberg before this battle was finished.

Tom and Gunner had been watching the seas rise all day. The wind had been increasing in the direction of the storm, and this had not helped the ships that were trying to push against the icebergs.

Tom thought to himself, *If the wind could push a big ship, then it must be helping to push these gigantic icebergs.*

Tom finished his thought as Gunner spoke out to the co-pilot and said, "We are full. It's time to disconnect."

Gunner then spoke to the tanker pilot on the radio and started a countdown, "Three, two, one, disconnect."

As the coast guard plane disconnected, there was a little jolt and they could feel more air drag on the aircraft, which began to slow them down. Tom thought to himself, *That was easy enough.*

Gunner said to the tanker pilot, "Everything is A-OK. Perfect disconnect, thank you and have a safe flight. Over and out."

Gunner turned the plane and began to descend. He could see smoke coming from a freighter that looked to be 150 feet long. As they got closer, Gunner showed Tom that there were two fire boats pouring water on the freighter while one tugboat was pulling it backward away from the iceberg. Tom could see another tugboat that had tied itself to the bow of the freighter and was beginning to turn the freighter. The tugboat that was behind the freighter slowed to allow the other tugboat in front to turn it. Tom and Gunner watched as the tugboats skillfully maneuvered the freighter. The tugboat that was at the stern of the fighter let go of his lines, and the other tugboat at the bow of the freighter toke over control. Tom nudged Gunner and said, "Those sailors really know what they're doing". Gunner explained to Tom that the fireboats would stay with the freighter until the fire was out or until they were clear of the icebergs.

Tom said to Gunner, "Those navy boys really know what they're doing. It looks like a traffic jam in a big metropolitan city in front of the iceberg. How could they possibly keep track of all those ships at the same time and keep them from running into one another? There must be a thousand ships in front of that iceberg. From here, it doesn't even look like they know which direction they are going, I see ship after ship being placed with their bow to the iceberg. How many ships do you think it will take to slow this iceberg down?"

Gunner replied, "I don't know, but from the reports I have heard over the radio, there are about two thousand ships pushing the icebergs and another thousand being escorted to their positions. The reports have also said that there could be as many as twenty thousand ships on their way and will arrive within the next ten to fifteen hours."

Tom said, "Well how in the world can they keep track of that many ships?"

"That really isn't as big of a problem as you might think. Remember, there are two aircraft carriers, one at the east and one at the west end of this iceberg. The Navistar Systems, which are satellites, can track every ship and plot its position, its course, and its speed. When you have the entire navy at your disposal, you're talking about thousands of engineers, computer experts, and satellite navigational experts. You see, it really isn't a big problem keeping track of all of the ships. The problem is trying to keep them all afloat and out of trouble," Gunner replied.

Just then Gunner heard a mayday from a cruise ship. Her position was thirty miles west from Gunner's plane. The ship's captain said that they had lost their starboard engine and they were bucking away from the iceberg. The captain also said that the navy controller told the cruise ship to keep backing and there would be help within five minutes. Gunner turned the plane and headed for the cruise ship. In just a few minutes, Gunner and Tom could see the cruise ship about one mile in front of the iceberg.

Gunner pointed just west of the cruise ship and said, "Tom, look! There's, a destroyer that is about two minutes from the cruise ship, and she's moving full speed."

The cruise ship captain had told Gunner that there were no passengers aboard—only a crew of eighty-five. Tom and Gunner could see the destroyer pull alongside the cruise ship until both of the ship bows were attached. Then they could see the destroyer tie itself to the cruise ship and began to turn the cruise ship around.

It took about five minutes, and both ships were heading south away from the icebergs at a very good speed. All of the crew on the coast guard plane were cheering and shouting at the top of their lungs.

"Gunner, what a crew you have!" Tom marveled.

Back on board the aircraft carrier the USS *Ranger*, Lydia and Jerry were in the mess hall at the captain's table with Admiral Norstrum.

"Is everything to your satisfaction in your quarters?" Admiral Norstrum asked.

Lydia spoke out excitedly, "If I hadn't landed on this aircraft carrier about a half an hour ago, I would swear that we were in a penthouse overlooking the sea. My quarters are so lovely it is hard to believe that we are on board a ship. Jerry, did you know that my quarters have a sauna and a sunken tub?"

Jerry smiled at Lydia and turned toward the admiral. "Sir, what's happening at the storm?"

Lydia broke in and said to Jerry, "Didn't you hear what I said?"

"Of course I did," replied Jerry. "It is just that my mind is fixed on the storm and I just cannot seem to think of anything else."

Admiral Norstrum said, "Okay, Jerry, after dinner we will check out everything that is going on with the storm and the iceberg!"

Just then the waiters came with the food and dinner began.

Meanwhile at the storm, the F14s, and F18s were busy continuing to keep the holes in the wall opened. Each plane flew and fired a missile and left, just to return in the next four to five minutes. They had to repeat this tactic over and over again. They could not afford these holes in the ice wall to close up. Until the water in the tornado had completely dissipated, there would be a continuing firing of missiles. Weather reports from the north and south in the Pacific Ocean reported high winds, thunderstorms, and rain storms all moving in the direction of "the Storm from Hell."

CHAPTER 10

After dinner, Admiral Norstrum introduced Lydia to a woman by the name of Patricia Manning, captain of the air defense aboard the USS *Ranger*. Lydia asked Ms. Manning if she was a pilot on board the USS *Ranger*.

"Yes! I sure am," replied Patricia. "I fly a Hawkeye airborne early warning aircraft on board the *Ranger*. Would you like a quick tour?"

Lydia replied, "Yes, Patricia, I would."

"Well, Lydia, you can call me Patty. Patricia is much too formal. Well, let's say our good-bye to Admiral Norstrum and Jerry, and let us tour aboard the *Ranger*."

Lydia and Captain Manning walked slowly through the USS *Ranger* as they began to get aquatinted with each other. Patty said, "Lydia have you ever been on an aircraft carrier before?"

Lydia replied, "Well no. This is the first time."

Lydia and Patty walked and talked for over two hours. They finally ended up at the flight deck.

"Would you like to see my little Hawkeye, Lydia? She isn't the best on the ship, but she sure can see the farthest in the air. I have a full computer system on board and can literally see everything for over two hundred miles in each direction."

Lydia said, "This Hawkeye is no bigger than the Albatross I was in just a few days ago. Jerry and I went right into the center of the storm. Of course your plane is much newer, and I'm sure has a lot more power. This has been the most exciting time of my life."

"Well it can get even more exciting. Why don't you come with me on my next flight out? Do you know anything about computers?" asked Patty.

"Yes, in fact I ran all the computers on the Albatross when we went in to the storm, and we brought back a mountain of information on these storms," Lydia bragged.

"Well, Lydia, it's getting late," said Patty. "We'd better find the boys and make plans for our flight for tomorrow morning."

Lydia and Patty made their way back to where the boys were, and Lydia was very excited and started to tell Jerry everything she experienced in the last few hours. Lydia asked the admiral if it would be okay if she went with Patty in the morning.

Admiral Norstrum replied, "Of course, Jerry and I are going to take a tour of the iceberg also. Maybe you can get to sleep and we'll all start out fresh in the morning."

It was 10:00 p.m. When Jerry and Lydia fell asleep, they both slept deeply and soundly. When they were awakened at 4:00 a.m., they thought to themselves that they never had such a good night's sleep.

Must be the sea air, Jerry thought to himself as he took his time showering, shaving, and getting dressed. *Lydia has to do all of the girl things also*, Jerry thought.

At 4:45 a.m., Jerry met Lydia in the mess hall.

Jerry said, "Lydia, I had the best sleep and I'm ready to go. How about you?"

"Well if you must know, I really didn't want to get out of my bed. After all, after this day, we will know if everything we have done will be worth it. You will know if it will stop the storm," Lydia replied.

"So this should be quite a day," Jerry said, and he smiled pleasantly toward Lydia.

"You're smiling again, Jerry. I like it when you smile. You look so handsome." Lydia blushed.

As they ate breakfast with the admiral, they talked about the day's events, and the admiral filled them in on everything that had happened through the night. Admiral Norstrum told them that there were almost four thousand ships with their bow to the 'berg, so to say. They hadn't lost one single ship during the night, and frankly, that was very good news. When everyone had finished breakfast,

Lydia told Jerry that she was going with Patty and would see him later.

Patty took Lydia to her ready room to prepare for their flight. First they were briefed on what to expect and what was to be expected from them on this flight. They proceeded to the dressing rooms and put on their flight suits. As they were getting ready, Lydia noticed that Patty was very muscular from all her working out. Patty was a very petite woman but strong.

Lydia asked Patty, "Have you had many boyfriends? Or should I say do you ever have problems with your boyfriends?"

"Well, not much," replied Patty. "I mean, I don't need a stick or anything," she chuckled to herself. "I don't have that many, and the ones I date now, I really don't have the time for them. What about you, Lydia? It looks like there is something going on with you and Jerry. I mean, the way you two look at each other, you can almost feel the sparks."

"Well honestly, Patty," exclaimed Lydia, "I just met Jerry three days ago at the beginning of this storm. There is something about him. Oh, I don't know. He is so wonderful, good-looking, and I have to admit I am highly attracted to him. I feel like a little schoolgirl when I am around him, and I hope it's not that obvious."

"Well, it is that obvious," Patty replied.

They finished dressing and were on their way to the plane. The flight crew had just finished preparing the plane and briefed Captain Manning about the flight. Patty and Lydia climbed aboard the plane, buckled themselves in, and Lydia could hear everything that was going on between Captain Manning and the flight tower. The plane was maneuvered into position and everything was ready. Lydia could see the flagman from the cockpit window. He started moving his flag in a circular motion. The engine started revving up, and it seemed like it was taking forever. Suddenly the flagman dropped his flag down, and the plane leaped forward so fast that Lydia's head shot back hard against the seat and she could not seem to move. She sensed the plane slowly slowing down, and it seemed as if everything was in slow motion. It felt as if the plane was ready to stop. What a trip! Then the plane seemed to catch up with itself, and the force of the engines seemed to take hold again.

What a strange sensation, thought Lydia.

As Patty was turning the plane in a circular motion, Lydia looked over her right shoulder, and she could see the *Ranger*. As Lydia looked forward, she could see the iceberg and all of the ships with their bow to the 'berg.

There was a distress call from a 360-foot container ship from the southwest hurricane. They reported that there was so much damage and loss that they could hardly hold course. By the time a helicopter reached the container ship and finally rescued the crew, it had been decided to sink the ship so that it would not cause a problem with the storm wall. After the rescue, they placed a homing device on board the ship for the air force to home in on.

Admiral Norstrum said to Jerry as he filled him in on the events of the night before, "Stand by me, Jerry, and listen.

"There is a fleet one hundred and thirty-five navy ships approaching the Hawaiian Islands from the Atlantic Fleet, and I have ordered them to stand by on the lee side of the island. They could not reach the storm's position before 1300 hours today. That is the estimated time that all of the ships will pull away from the iceberg and should give us two hours to clear the iceberg. If we are correct, the iceberg will reach the shallow water relief at 1600 hours, which is seven p.m. and just before dark." Admiral Norstrum continued by saying that the water in the storm should be less than fifty feet above sea level at that time.

As Jerry and Admiral Norstrum boarded the helicopter to take a tour of the iceberg, Jerry could see the iceberg in the distance. The *Ranger* had gotten much closer to the iceberg during the night. As they left the carrier, Jerry said to Admiral Norstrum that it looked like a naval convoy because there were so many ships.

"I have never seen so many ships in one place at the same time. There were so many different kinds of ships and so much activity around the leading edge of the iceberg that it looks like a beehive," said Jerry.

As they surveyed the iceberg, Admiral Norstrum heard a report about the container ship and told Jerry that the ship had lost about half of its cargo already and was listing to starboard fifteen degrees. They had a hard time picking up the crew off of the container ship. The seas in side of the number one hurricane were fairly common, but the fifteen-degree listing was making the rescue very difficult for the rescue teams.

They had been in the air for about an hour when Admiral Norstrum said to Jerry, "We only have four hours left to slow down the iceberg. This will be the most crucial part of Storm Safe. We will only have six hours to get all of the ships out of the way of the leading edge of the iceberg at a safe distance."

For the next two hours, Jerry and Admiral Norstrum surveyed the iceberg and the ships. They were both impressed with the sight of this gigantic icebergs and the speed of this ice river that was moving at such a fast rate.

Just then Admiral Norstrum said to Jerry, "Can you imagine? Our engineers have told me that there are millions of horsepower collectively in all of those ships that are pushing against the iceberg, and we can only hope to slow down this overgrown iceberg. In all of my years in the navy, I have never seen so much power used to try to control something this big. I am impressed with all the navy's technology and ability to even try something on this scale. To top it all off, we are succeeding. We have slowed the iceberg down, and we will reach our goal of saving ten hours. You know, Jerry, this is one of the navy's finest accomplishments. We have made history in these past few days, and no matter what happens, this will be America's finest hour."

As they were approaching the aircraft carrier *Ranger*, Jerry thought, *It looks like they might have a chance to stop this storm after all.*

After seeing all of the cooperation from so many different countries and their ships with their captains, it gave Jerry a renewed hope for mankind.

After landing on the *Ranger*, Admiral Norstrum and Jerry went to the control room to find out all of the latest news. When they got to the control room, they found it buzzing like a beehive. By the time Jerry and the admiral got back to the carrier, all hell had broken loose. The seas had gotten rougher and had risen to thirty-five—to forty-foot swells. With only four hours to go before the ships could break away from the iceberg, it seemed like everything had made a turn for the worst at the iceberg.

To make things worse, Captain Patty Manning and Lydia were about four hundred miles south east of the *Ranger* and reporting a typhoon that they were in the middle of. A typhoon, as it is called in the Pacific North hemisphere, is a hurricane. Their report was that it was small but growing, with winds of 160 miles per hour and moving at a speed of twenty-five miles per hour directly toward the storm from hell. One hundred and twenty five miles in diameter. There were seven ships in its path and two ships caught inside sending SOS calls. Admiral Norstrum immediately sent four helicopters and a search and rescue plane to that location.

Just then the shuttle called to inform the *Ranger* that there were three hurricanes that had just formed in the vicinity of the southern portion of the Pacific: just off the coast of Indonesia north of Australia at 135.41 East and 6.08 North; another at 145.28 East by 1.57 North; and the last one at 60.52 East by 1.08 North. They were moving in a northeast direction toward the *Ranger*.

In a report from Edwards Air Force Base, it was confirmed two different hurricanes, one west of South America just of Chile at 87.02 West by 28.04 South and the other 110.30 West by 24.38 South moving in a northwest direction

Gunner and Tom radioed in to Admiral Norstrum. "There is one more hurricane that is a thousand miles northwest just off of Russia at 163.35 East by 50.36 North. But this storm is a monster. The hurricane is two hundred miles in diameter with 175 miles an hour winds and moving in a southeast direction at a speed of sixty miles per hour. The only good thing about this storm is that there are no ships in its path that are in danger."

Admiral Norstrum looked at Jerry and said, "It looks like all hell is breaking loose."

Jerry said to the admiral, "It isn't that bad. The only storm that we have to deal with is the one at hand. I have expected this to happen. You see, with all the high pressure caused by the tornado and three hurricanes, I expected this to happen days ago. We are just hours away from completion now, and the only other storm that could affect us is the hurricane that Captain Manning and Lydia are at. The other storms are too far away to bother us at this time, but it doesn't look good."

Admiral Norstrum ordered search and rescue planes to all of the seven new storms and ordered Captain Manning and Captain Gunner back to the *Ranger*.

By the time Captain Manning and Lydia were back on board on the *Ranger*, everything had calmed down a little. Gunner and Tom had arrived now, and they all met in the mess hall at the captain's table. Lydia, Tom, Gunner, and Patty were all asking questions.

Then Jerry spoke, "Okay, it is all going to be all right. There is only one other problem that can affect our operation, and that is the hurricane to the southeast off Mexico that is 137.44 West and 25.36 North that Captain Manning and Lydia found. I think our time frame is still intact. Admiral Norstrum has ordered all of the ships to pull away from the iceberg, and we only have six hours to go. So let's eat lunch and get a couple of hours of rest. We will need it. We have done everything we can do. All we can do is pray that everything we have done will work."

All of the questions stopped, and a silence fell at the captain's table as everyone ate his or her lunch. There was a reverence in the mess hall Jerry noted as he finished his lunch.

Jerry's thoughts went to a much higher plane as he considered all of the events that had happened in the past week. *Have all of these things I have learned in my life been coming to this very day? Has there been a higher power in my life directing me to this day? Can one man really make a difference in all of humanity?* Jerry knew that no matter what happened, after today, his life would never be the same. Jerry's life had been touched by so many other people, and he understood that he had touched thousands of people and neither they nor he would be the same.

For the next five hours, Jerry was with Admiral Norstrum in the command room watching all news of the ships moving away from the iceberg. The slowest ships were ordered away from the iceberg first so they would have time to clear the iceberg before the iceberg moved over the shallow water reef. There were seven thousand ships in front of the iceberg when the admiral ordered the evacuation. Five thousand of the ships had their bows to the 'berg, with two thousand escort and rescue ships. Jerry asked the admiral what had happened to the other nine thousand ships that were going to be here to help. The admiral answered that they just couldn't make it in time.

"When we saw that they would not make it in time, we turned them around and headed them away from the storm. I also ordered them to move away from the storm as fast as possible and to expect a tidal wave so when I give the word they would have time to turn around and head into it. Those that could find shelter were told to do so," Admiral Norstrum stated.

The admiral gave the order that any ship that had trouble keeping away from the iceberg would be evacuated immediately and sunk. Time was running short, and they could not afford any complications that could compromise this operation. The admiral told Jerry that they were ahead of schedule and that at five p.m., all ships would be clear of the iceberg.

In this operation, they had only lost three ships and forty-three lives.

"We really have been fortunate, you know," Jerry said to the admiral. "This could have been a very bad situation."

All ships had been ordered to head north of the iceberg by the admiral and to stay behind the iceberg for shelter from the storm or a tidal wave. At least they would have some protection in the command room. Jerry and the admiral had been watching all of the reports of the ships at the icebergs and the reports from the storm itself. The storm wall was still intact, and the water level was now less than two hundred feet above sea level. Everything seemed to be going well, with no complications. Jerry hoped that with all things that had gone wrong in the past few days, nothing went wrong now.

Jerry's thoughts began to run wild. *What if these other hurricanes start another storm from hell?*

Then when Jerry dismissed his thought, he remembered the high pressure caused by this storm. Jerry knew that the high pressure would definitely form other storms and thought how really lucky they were that they hadn't started before now.

Tom and Gunner were back in the air with less than an hour before the iceberg ran over the shallow water reef.

Meanwhile, the news media all over the world had been broadcasting reports about the storm and the iceberg live most of the time with help from the navy. After all, this was the most catastrophic event to happen on the Earth in all of recorded history. Many people believed that this may be the end of the world.

Churches had gone crazy all over the world with their prophesying of the rapture and the coming of Jesus Christ.

A lot of churches were half-full of people giving their life to Christ. People were crying in the streets, "The end is coming, the end is coming!"

TV preachers were broadcasting and saying, "I told you the end was coming, and now that it is here maybe you will believe me."

Banks and entire governments had closed their doors. It seemed that the whole world was glued to their TV or radio listening to the news. The world was at a standstill waiting to see what would happen.

Captain Manning and Lydia had been watching the news. But being close at hand to the storm and what was really happening, Lydia and Patty were not as worried as the world was in this. Things didn't seem so bad; in fact, they were looking very good from Patty and Lydia's point of view. If everything went as planned, they should be back to normal in a few weeks.

"Your boyfriend Jerry really has things under control and has thought of everything. He really is a clever man and quite handsome, I might add," said Patty. "You are a very lucky girl, Lydia, to make a catch like Jerry."

Lydia blushed slightly as she remarked to Patty, "I know, and I love it."

CHAPTER 11

All of the ships had left the iceberg and gotten out of the way and out of the area. As the iceberg began to move straight over the shallow reef, the ice water river began to flow faster until the water turned white. In the next ten minutes, the icebergs moved ever the shallow reefs and began to cover the reef. The water increased in speed as the icebergs and the reef distance closed.

Tom was in the coast guard plane with Gunner and witnessed what was happening as the iceberg moved over the shallow-water reef. From their advantage, they could see the most spectacular show that any man had ever been able to attest to. There were great fountains of water being shot out from the front of this iceberg that sprayed into the air. There were some as high as two thousand or even three thousand feet under enormous pressure, with ice water and ice crystals with chunks of ice as big as a car. This was happening over a thirty-mile stretch where the river flowed over the underwater reef and under the iceberg. As this shower of ice and water clouded the sun, there was an incredible light show, with rainbows and colors that were so unexplainable.

"I have never seen the likes of this before," said Tom. "It's like seeing a geyser,"

There were rivers of water shooting straight out in front of the iceberg. Some were like big jets, pushing them one or two miles in front of the iceberg, some as high as an aircraft carrier. For thirty miles in every direction from the iceberg, you could see fountains and streams and rivers and fantastic-looking fountains of icy water with a spectacular spectrum of colors.

The sound from the iceberg, as it started to ground on the reef, was almost deafening. Tom and Gunner were flying at five thousand feet and thirty miles in front of the iceberg. The ice and reef colliding and tearing each other apart sounded like thunder crackling and breaking for a hundred miles as the gigantic iceberg moved over the reef. The thunderous sound from under the sea had mothballed the sound of Gunner's four great engines on his airplane. It was like a battlefield, with everyone firing at the same time in the middle of a thunderstorm. It sounded like being at a rock concert and standing next to the biggest speakers you have ever seen, and it seemed to go right through you. The sight of this gigantic iceberg dancing was unbelievable. You had to keep in mind that this iceberg was over one hundred miles wide and two hundred miles long and in places one thousand feet above sea level. In most spots, the iceberg was one hundred feet below the water. As the iceberg grounded itself on the reef, it bounced and swayed. It wiggled and jiggled like a harpooned whale trying to break free from the death grip of whale killers. The iceberg finally came to rest over the reef. With a final burst and launch, the river gave its last bit of energy and then gave up. The river finally changed directions. If you could imagine for a minute this happening all at the same time for about twenty minutes! It looked like the Fourth of July from the entire United States of America all on the California coast. A light show and fireworks display with the sound of thunder and with breaking ice like the sound of breaking glass. So deafening was the sound that it went right through you to the very core of your being,

Tom sighed. *This is the most spectacular show I have ever seen.*

Back on the USS *Ranger*, Jerry and the admiral were delighted and jumping with joy as the iceberg settled and turned the direction of the ice river. The river stopped flowing all at once in the direction of the storm and began to flow in an eastern direction toward California. In all of their excitement, Jerry and the admiral had forgotten about the storm for a moment—that was until reports started coming in about the storm wall from spotter planes and helicopters. As Jerry and the admiral listened to the reports, they could no longer hear human voices, only crackling noises like breaking glass and thunder coming over the speakers at the command center. The sound was so loud that it blew out four speakers in the command room. After about a minute, Jerry could hear voices on the radio as they began to explain just what was going on with the wall. There were five or six reports coming in at the same time, with so much static and emotion that Jerry had to focus in on only one report to make sense of it all.

The very first thing Jerry could hear and understand was that the wall had collapsed. It took about three minutes before one pilot had a clear enough transmission to understand just what he was saying. All of the reports were garbled and sporadic. Nothing seemed to make sense at first, and panic set in from the sides of the storm wall where pilots were stationed. Jerry was picking up some reports from ships, from planes, and from helicopters. Nothing made sense, and nothing was clear. Then was a sound of thunder that was so loud that even when you held your hands over your ears, the sound just went through your hands, through your ears, and even through your bones. It was at least five minutes before Jerry could hear anything. Everyone in the command room was in pain from the sound of thunder going through their bodies. Then the admiral grabbed Jerry by the arm and turned him around.

"Jerry," said the admiral, "you have to hear this."

The admiral led Jerry to an ensign receiving a message from a fighter pilot. As they put the earphones on, Jerry could hear the report clearly.

"The ice wall has collapsed, and as it collapsed, it has thrown a wave of water almost five miles high and twenty-five to thirty miles outward. It has come out from the lower wall in every direction. From my position, all I can see is white foam for at least fifty miles in both directions of the wall position when it fell. I have lost contact with the X1 and have not been able to locate her. I fear she is lost. Wait, there is something different. It looks like a giant foam wave is forming at the location of the wall and moving outward from the storm. I will report anymore findings as soon as possible. Over."

For the next thirty minutes, Jerry and the admiral listened to reports from pilots all around the storm. Then finally there came a confirmation from a search and rescue helicopter that was inside the storm when the wall collapsed. The water level at the time of collapse was forty feet above sea level. There was joy and jubilation and singing in the control room. Everyone in the control room knew that a forty-foot tidal wave, by the time it reached shore, would only be about twenty feet. By this time, Lydia and Captain Manning had returned from debriefing their flight then joined Jerry and the admiral in the control room, where they were jumping for joy. The next report brought tears to Jerry's eyes. The report said that the three hurricanes were beginning to move away from the beaten tornado. Jerry was actually sobbing when Lydia found him. Jerry was crumpled on the floor and sobbing like a baby, tears of joy streaming down his face in an uncontrollable release. Lydia could not help herself as she joined in with a joyful flood of tears streaming down her own face. Before long, the entire control room was flooded with tears. The relief from all of the pressure even moved Admiral Norstrum to tears of his own.

The sun was setting as Lydia and Jerry stepped out on the flight deck of the aircraft carrier *Ranger*. The sea was very upset with all of the storms. With thirty—to forty-foot swells from the storm, a mist covered the *Ranger* like a blanket covered a bed. With the icebergs in sight, clouds of every shape created a light show. Colors shined through the clouds, and rainbows flowed through the mist.

Jerry then said to Lydia, "Lydia, this must be the most passionate evening in all of my life."

Jerry then stumbled at words he was about to say to Lydia. "Lydia, I think I'm falling in love with you."

Lydia appeared to be taken aback, but then replied, "You better be, because I have already fallen in love with you."

As they turned toward each other, Jerry looked at Lydia and could see a rainbow of colors dancing in her eyes. Jerry leaned over to kiss her. Lydia tilted her head back slightly to consent to his kiss.

It was dark now, and Jerry and Lydia returned to the control room. Everyone there was very tired after this very hard day. The admiral informed everyone that there was a tidal wave of about forty feet on the way to the coast. It was reported from one of the planes.

"Just when we thought this was over," said the admiral. "I know everyone here is tired. We'll keep on top of this tidal wave. You need to eat and get some rest. If there are any changes, we'll wake you all up immediately."

Admiral Norstrum ordered a change of shift. "Tomorrow will be another day. Go and get some food and a good rest. You all deserve it."

Jerry and Lydia met the admiral for dinner at the captain's table. Shortly after being seated, Tom and Gunner arrived and joined them. They all ate slowly as they shared the day's events with each other—the color shows, the victories, and all the hard work. Admiral Norstrum could see by the look on all of their faces that everyone was tired.

"That was a good dinner," the admiral said. "I think I am going to retire to my quarters. I think everyone here would like to do the same."

Jerry, Lydia, Tom, and Gunner agreed, and they all retired to their quarters.

At 4:30 a.m., Jerry awoke and called the mess hall and had them bring him a pot of coffee. When the coffee arrived at his room, he got out of bed and put on a robe and went to a sitting room that had a bay window overlooking the flight deck adjacent to his bedroom. Pulling back the drapes, he could see planes taking off and landing. Jerry sat back and relaxed as he finished his first cup of coffee. There was a knock on the door. Jerry got up to answer the door, and as he opened the door, he could see Lydia wearing a robe just like his. It was a white terrycloth robe, and on her it touched the floor. Jerry's face lit up like a Christmas tree as he said: "Well, it looks like we have the same good taste in clothes."

Lydia laughed and said, "I knew I smelled coffee."

"Yes," Jerry answered as he closed the door behind Lydia. "I'll go and pour you a cup."

Lydia went straight to the sitting room and sat down on the couch overlooking the flight deck. As Jerry brought her a cup of coffee, he could see that Lydia looked well rested and fresh. Lydia had put on a very dull blush and a light rose-colored lipstick that glistened like diamonds sparkling on the face of water in the moonlight. Lydia had a smile that you could die for. Jerry gave her the cup of coffee and sat down beside her. Lydia took one sip of the coffee and put the cup down on the coffee table in front of her. Then she took Jerry's cup and put it next to hers on the table. Lydia turned toward Jerry and threw her arms around him and gave him a kiss that shot his blood pressure up at least a hundred points. After that passionate kiss, Lydia turned back to the coffee table and picked up Jerry's coffee and handed it to him. She picked up her own coffee cup and took another sip.

Without a word, Lydia leaned over and gave Jerry another small kiss and said, "So how did you sleep? Like a baby I hope."

Jerry replied, "The best night's sleep I have had in years."

As they sat there in the sitting room, they overlooked the flight deck with the lights reflecting through the room. Lydia and Jerry leaned against each other as they sipped their coffee. They felt very comfortable together. It must have been at least ten minutes and not a word had been spoken. They just sipped their coffee and felt the reverence of each other's company. The sky turned a light gray, with a bit of purple just before sunrise. Lydia stood up and asked Jerry if he would like another cup of coffee.

Jerry said, "I would love one." As Lydia walked across the floor, Jerry thought to himself that she looked like a princess floating on a cloud. She brought back the coffee and placed the cup on the coffee table in front of Jerry. She again sat down next to Jerry, and they watched the sunrise as it reflected against the iceberg with its brilliant colors dancing across the water.

After Jerry and Lydia finished their coffee, Lydia got up and with a big smile on her face said, "I think it's time that I go and get dressed for the day." Jerry walked Lydia to the door.

"This is the most pleasant morning that I can remember," said Jerry. "I will see you in the mess hall in about thirty minutes."

Jerry gave Lydia a small kiss on the lips and Lydia said, "Thank you for the coffee and a beautiful sunrise."

Jerry met the admiral in the mess hall at the captain's table. The admiral had a smile from ear to ear as Jerry approached the table. Jerry said to the admiral, "You look very happy today."

"I am," replied the admiral.

Just then Tom, Lydia, and Gunner arrived at the captain's table. After they were all seated, Admiral Norstrum said, "I have good news for all of you. This morning about thirty minutes ago, the three hurricanes that caused the Storm from Hell have been downgraded to tropical storms. The tidal wave has caused a lot of damage to shipping, but so far nothing we can't handle. We lost three of our experimental ships with no survivors. Fourteen other ships have been lost during the night, ranging from freighters to tugboats. The tidal wave is two hours from the iceberg and is less than forty feet now. It will be hitting the Hawaiian Islands in about the same time. The president of the United States of America wants all of you back at Edwards Air Force Base by twelve hundred hours today. I will be accompanying you, and you won't need to worry about all of your things. They are being packed as we speak. After we eat, we will be leaving for Edwards Air Force Base. Our plane will be ready for takeoff in less than an hour. I have taken the liberty to bring Captain Manning with us, so let us enjoy our meals and celebrate our victory. Most of the danger is over."

After their meal, Jerry, Lydia, Tom, Gunner, Admiral Norstrum, and Captain Manning were escorted to a small two engine jet airplanes on the flight deck of the *Ranger*. The plane was ready for takeoff, and it didn't take long until the small company was in the air. The plane was a Lear jet that seated eight people and flew very fast. After leaving the flight deck behind, they flew over the iceberg and toward the tidal wave. The pilot brought the plane down to about two hundred feet above the water so they could see the tidal wave. Then, the pilot climbed to forty thousand feet and pushed the throttles full. The flight took only two hours, and they landed at Edwards Air Force base.

When they got off of the plane, Larry Walsh and Colonel Thompson met them. There was a brass band and about a thousand reporters from the news media with brass from the military. There were people from the government and civilians. It was a real fanfare. Jerry thought to himself, *Hail the conquering heroes.*

There was a ceremony for Jerry, Lydia, and Tom with flags, flowers, and praises for their fight against the storm. After the ceremony, Jerry, Lydia, and Tom were escorted to the conference room with Larry and Colonel Thompson. Colonel Thompson told Tom of his concern for Gunner's plane in Long Beach and gave him orders to have Gunner get his plane. Tom thanked Colonel Thompson and laughed as he left to go find Gunner. By the time Tom found Gunner, Colonel Thompson had already given Gunner his orders. They were in the air and on their way to Long Beach within the hour. On the way, Gunner flew directly to the coast and then followed the coast southward all the way to Long Beach. Gunner and Tom had not spent this much time together in fifteen years since they were in the service together. As they followed the coast, Gunner and Tom were talking about the fact that the coast looked just like it did six days ago. Everything seemed to be back to normal.

"When the tidal wave hits, most everything in the coastal cities could be destroyed," said Tom. "In the next one and one half days, things could get bad again." As they reached Long Beach, everything looked normal. After landing, Gunner ordered his crew to help load his plane with all of his belongings.

If the tidal wave hits, this would all be underwater and ruined, thought Tom. *Maybe even the buildings won't be here after the tidal wave hits.*

Tom and Gunner decided to leave for Edwards Air Force base.

CHAPTER 12

After the news conference, Jerry, Lydia, and Larry were all watching different news clips from around the world. Suddenly, Larry collapsed in a heap on the floor. Lydia panicked but then just kneeled by her father and said a prayer and yelled for help. Doctors and nurses came from everywhere. They covered Larry with a blanket and then took him to an adjoining room. It was like they were expecting this to happen. When Lydia and Jerry entered the adjoining room, Jerry could see that it was an operating room. As they watched the doctors work on Lydia's dad, Admiral Norstrum and Colonel Thompson began to talk to them.

"Lydia," said Colonel Thompson, "this kind of thing happens all of the time. Your father will be okay. We have the best stress cardiac doctors in the world here at the conference. The stress that we have all been under can't help but to get to us all at times. This has happened nine times in the past three days, and we expect it to happen a lot more before it is over."

A doctor came over to Lydia and told her that her dad was okay.

"Lydia," said the doctor, "your dad needs a rest. Come on over and see for yourself."

They walked to Larry's bedside.

Larry looked up at Lydia and said, "It is okay, honey, I feel fine. It just took the breath out of me. It took the wind out of my sails."

After about fifteen minutes with her dad, the doctor escorted Lydia and Jerry to another room where there were reclining chairs and couches with a lot of pictures on the walls. After Lydia and Jerry sat down on a couch, the doctor began to explain just what was going to happen.

"Ms. Walsh," said the doctor, "in less than one hour, you and your dad will be in a resort in the High Sierras, sitting on lawn chairs at the edge of a lake in a beautiful setting in a most relaxing atmosphere. You'll be coming back after a short stay, but your Father will stay for about a week under close supervision. You can fly there at least once a day if you want to see him. Your conversation has to be very lighthearted. And please keep it to that. You see, under high stress management, we just want your father to forget about the past few days. This is a very hard thing to do for a man who is so dedicated to his job and helping others. The rest of the times you are with him, enjoy yourself. Try to separate yourself from the past few days and imagine that you and your dad are on a vacation. This treatment is all about resting and relaxing. That is the main theme. Your father has no cardiac problems at all. High stress and very little rest have caused this. I am sure that you could use a little rest yourself, so please take advantage of this time and consider it to be a vacation paid for by the government."

Jerry said to Lydia, "Don't worry about anything. I will be right here when you get back."

Lydia gave Jerry a kiss, and then she left with the doctor for the transport plane. Jerry went back to the conference room, where he met up with Tom and Gunner. They asked about Larry and Lydia. Jerry told them all about it and left it at that. He then told Tom and Gunner that Lydia would be back in a few hours.

Lydia and Larry were escorted to a small seaplane about the size of Tom's but newer. It was like a hospital inside, and the flight only took about twenty-five minutes. Then they landed on a very secluded lake.

Lydia thought to herself, *This is the most beautiful lake I have ever seen.*

Lydia could see no roads or cars, just half a dozen log cabins nestled majestically on a lake with a small dock.

The landing was very smooth, Lydia thought as they were pulling up to the dock.

Lydia could see about a dozen chairs near the lake with a couple of tables and umbrellas. There were only four men sitting by the lake, and they looked very comfortable being attended by two nurses. Two other nurses and a doctor met Lydia and Larry on the dock. They were escorted to the largest log cabin, which seemed to be the main hospital but had the ambiance of a beautiful resort. The setting was so relaxing and beautiful that any artist would feel like he or she could stay and paint for the rest of his or her life.

After about an hour, Lydia found herself boarding the seaplane with no reservations about leaving her father. She knew that Larry was in very capable hands and would get a well-deserved rest. As the seaplane skipped across the lake and took off, circling the resort, they climbed out of this beautiful valley.

Lydia then thought to herself, *The next time I come back here, I'll bring Jerry and we'll have a picnic with Dad. I'm sure Jerry could use some rest just as much as I can.*

On the flight back to Edwards Air Force Base, Lydia reflected on the past few days.

Lydia thought, *How lucky I am to have gotten into an accident with Jerry Turner at the Jolly Roger.*

She thought about getting out of her car and yelling at Jerry like a tiger about to pounce on its prey and giggled.

It was a very short flight, and as they landed at Edwards, Lydia could see Jerry, Tom, and Gunner waiting for the plane to taxi up to them and stop. The boys were glad to see Lydia and escorted her to a conference room, from where they filled her in on all the latest news. Everyone seemed to be very happy and joyous as they entered the conference room. They escorted her to one of the larger TV screens, and they all took a seat and said to Lydia, "This will be the best part of all."

Lydia said, "Jerry, this is a report from the naval department. Let's watch it and see what they say."

Lydia's eyes were fixed on the giant screen.

"Hello. This is the US naval department, and we are reporting live via satellite. We are aboard the USS aircraft carrier *Ranger*, and this report has been put together to show the results of this gigantic storm system in the North Pacific Ocean that the world has been fighting for the past four days. We have helicopters flying over what is left from a tornado that was being powered by three hurricanes. The three hurricanes have dissipated, with winds less than fifty miles per hour, and are getting slower as we speak. As you can see, there seems to be a gigantic ice ring that is approximately five hundred miles in diameter and five miles thick bobbing like a cork in the middle of the ocean. This ice ring is sticking up out of the water about one hundred feet and has four hundred feet of ice below it.

"There are six holes in the wall of the iceberg, which we have continued to keep open, and at this hour, all of the water that was contained inside of the wall has been dissipated, and the inside water level is the same level as the outside water level. So you can see there is no more danger of a tidal wave being caused by this storm. The wave that we thought was a tidal wave was in reality a wave caused when the ice wall lost its power and fell into the ocean, causing a forty-foot ring of water that moved away from the storm. There is now no danger to the coastal cities of the Pacific Ocean. The holes in the ice ring have been made bigger and kept open by the navy and air force to allow oil cleanup crews to enter in and clean up all of the crude oil that was lost from the supertanker that was in the middle of the storm. This operation should take approximately three more days. The US navy will surround this gigantic ice ring to ensure safe shipping until the ice ring has melted. The US naval department has brought this report to you and we will keep you posted and updated on a regular basis."

Lydia was thrilled, to say the least. She threw her arms around Jerry and gave him a big kiss and said, "Jerry, you have to be the hero of all times."

Everyone in the conference room started cheering and clapping, and then began to sing, "For He's a Jolly Good Fellow." For the next three days, the reports continued, and plans were being made by the US government and dignitaries from a hundred different countries around the world, to honor these three heroes: Lydia Walsh, Tom Goodman, and Jerry Turner. Jerry and Lydia had the opportunity to spend the next three days getting to know one another better and were able to spend a lot of quality time together.

Tom and Gunner spent a lot of time together bringing each other up to date on all things that happened in their lives for the past fifteen years. Colonel Thompson and Admiral Norstrum were busy taking care of a thousand small details while they nurtured a new friendship that would last for the rest of their life. All of the brass in the US government and the president of the United States decided that they would honor these three heroes with a ticker-tape parade in New York City.

The next day, Lydia and Jerry boarded a small seaplane and flew to the lake where Larry Walsh had been recuperating. Jerry and Lydia were very happy as the plane landed on the water and taxied to the boat dock. As they reached the boat dock, they could see Larry waiting for them with a giant smile on his face. As Jerry and Lydia got out of the plane, she remarked to Jerry, "My dad sure is looking good and rested."

As Jerry and Lydia walked up the boat dock to meet Larry, Lydia said, "Jerry, we should spend the whole day here and get a little rest and relaxation ourselves."

Jerry replied, "Sounds like the best idea I've heard in the past couple of weeks."

Larry looked rested. In fact, Larry looked more rested than he had been in years. As Larry greeted Lydia with a big hug, he explained to her, "Lydia, honey, I haven't felt this good in years!"

Larry escorted Lydia and Jerry to a small, secluded beach away from the log cabins where there were three chairs with fishing poles and an ice cooler filled with sodas and iced tea.

Larry said to Jerry, "Sit down and let's take the rest of the day to get to know one another better and just relax and have some fun."

Lydia remarked, "Dad, you haven't talked like this in years. Usually, all you think about is working."

Larry replied, "I have had a lot of time to think the last few days, and maybe I've been working too hard. As a matter of fact, maybe I should retire and allow more time for fishing. Enough of that for now. Let's just relax and take it easy for the next few hours."

Jerry picked up a fishing pole that was next to his chair and put some bait on the hook and cast it out into the lake. Then he sat down. Before Jerry could speak a word, a fish took the hook, and Jerry fought the fish to the beach. Jerry turned to show off his catch to Lydia and Larry. In the next ten minutes, Jerry caught three more trout. They were rainbow trout and about ten inches long. Jerry was very excited, but he noticed that Larry hadn't caught a thing.

Without hesitation, he reached over and grabbed Larry's fishing pole and reel, saying, "Larry, the fish are biting very well. You must have lost your bait. I will put new bait on your line for you."

Larry did not say a word as Jerry pulled in Larry's line.

Jerry had a surprised look on his face when he found no hook at the end of Larry's line.

Jerry turned to Larry and said, "A fish must have taken your hook."

"No, I didn't put a hook or bait on my line just a senker because I didn't want to be bothered by the fish. It is just so beautiful here and so relaxing that it didn't seem to be important," Larry replied.

For the next four hours, Jerry didn't even bother to fish. The three of them just sat around and talked. A nurse came down to the lake to tell them it was lunchtime and escort them to the main cabin for lunch. Over lunch, they told Larry all the good news. Larry had good news of his own.

"Kids, this afternoon I am flying back to Edwards Air Force Base with you. The doctors say that I have recovered from the stress and I'm ready to accompany you back to the base."

Larry had a smile on his face from ear to ear. After they ate lunch, Larry said to Lydia and Jerry, "Why don't you kids take a walk around the lake? It takes about one and a half to two hours, and I'll be busy with the doctors as they give me the final once over. It really is a beautiful day, and I know you'll enjoy it."

Just then the doctor came and said, "Larry it's time for your physical." Larry got up from the table. He turned to Lydia and Jerry and said, "You kids have some fun now. I will see you in a few hours."

Jerry and Lydia got up and walked out the front door, heading for the lake. Larry watched them as they walked hand in hand toward the trail that leads around the lake.

It was a beautiful day, about eighty degrees in the sun with a brisk, almost chilling breeze blowing down from the surrounding mountains. It was the kind of day that when you stand in the shade you almost want to put on a jacket or a sweater. Jerry thought to himself that this was the kind of day that the Lord must have made for Adam and Eve in the Garden of Eden. The path was wide enough for three people to walk abreast and very well maintained, almost like a road, but there wasn't a tire print anywhere to be found, nor did they ever find any evidence of any motor vehicle. Lydia skipped and sometimes bolted ahead like a little schoolgirl to embrace some new treasure like a piece of driftwood or a squirrel running up a tree. She felt free and happy and full of excitement. This was a side of Lydia that Jerry hadn't seen and was very appealing—the ability to be as a little child, to be uninhibited and to cast aside all of the troubles of the world. Jerry hadn't felt that way for years. He was too caught up in his life of despair to even have fun.

This is very infectious, thought Jerry as he began to forget the troubles of the world. Jerry began to skip and run and play tag with Lydia as two schoolchildren would play in the schoolyard. Jerry missed this kind of feeling most of all. As Jerry and Lydia ran back and forth on the trail, they discovered many treasures as they played like little children. They forgot all about time.

Now this is what life should be all about, thought Lydia.

On the other side of the lake, there was a stream that ran into the lake with stepping stones placed in the stream so that you could walk across it without getting wet and without taking giant steps. As Lydia and Jerry were crossing the stream, she reached down with one hand and scooped up a handful of water and splashed it on Jerry. Then she turned and ran ahead of Jerry, taunting him to chase her. Jerry reached down with both hands and scooped up some water and began to chase Lydia. As Jerry caught up with Lydia, he splashed the water on her back. She was running, and Lydia squealed like a schoolgirl.

Lydia said, "That's not fair. You can run faster than I can."

She giggled and turned and threw her arms around Jerry, giving him a big kiss and lifting her feet up off the ground. After their embrace, they turned and walked hand in hand down the trail until they came upon two tree stumps in the lake that were sticking up out of the water. They were about six inches high and about two feet from the shore. Lydia ran ahead and jumped on top of one of the tree stumps and said to Jerry, "I bet you can't do this."

Jerry jumped on the other tree stump as Lydia reached down and splashed water on Jerry two or three times. She couldn't stop giggling. She jumped off of the stump and ran back to the trail. She stopped to rest by some wild flowers. As Jerry approached, he picked a bouquet of wild flowers and presented them to Lydia as he sat down beside her.

Lydia looked up at Jerry and said, "You're such a gentleman and quite handsome, if I may add."

Jerry looked lovingly at Lydia and said, "I have been writing a little poetry for you.

"Let me take you to the moon, the heavens have opened for two, as one we will waltz along the milky way as the glittering stars pale at your joyful smile, when our spirits intertwine we will shoot as a comet to the earth to cool our heated journey. We will splash into the sea, O my love our spirits joined and intertwined as one, as dolphins we shall dance across the sea and surf the waves before the Lord."

"Oh, Jerry," Lydia said as she threw her arms around his neck. "You really do love me."

Just then, they could hear an airplane, and looking up, they could see it was the seaplane about to make a landing. Lydia jumped to her feet and gave Jerry a slight nudge, which pushed him off his balance, as he fell backward and landed on his butt. Lydia turned and began to run, and with a giggle in her voice said, "Beat you to the plane!"

Jerry got up and began to chase Lydia, but by the time they reached the plane, Lydia was still ahead. Larry was standing by the dock as Lydia threw her arms around him and hid behind him from Jerry.

"Okay, you two kids. It's time to leave for Edwards Air Force Base," said Larry with a smile on his face.

They boarded the plane and flew back to Edwards Air Force Base, where they were greeted by Colonel Thompson, Admiral Norstrum, Tom, and Gunner. Colonel Thompson said, "We are running a little late, so we just have time to get to the plane. We are all flying to Washington DC, where we will have a meeting with the president."

They all got into the car and were driven to the plane. Tom, Lydia, and Jerry were surprised to see Air Force One, the president's airplane, waiting to take them to Washington.

When they landed in Washington DC, nobody got off the plane. The president and his wife and the vice president and his wife boarded the plane, and they left for New York City. After takeoff, Admiral Norstrum introduced the president, the vice president, and their wives to Jerry, Lydia, and Tom.

The president said, "I have had the pleasure of meeting these fine people. The pleasure, though, was very short and abrupt. Jerry, I have taken the liberty to put your ex-wife and children on an airplane for New York City. They will be meeting us at the hotel after we land. I do want them to see you honored by your country and the world. Tomorrow morning we will be in a motorcade driving down Broadway to Times Square in the heart of New York City. This parade will be given in your honor, all three of you. There will be a ceremony and a dedication after the parade.

"Lydia, you and Tom will be awarded a Medal of Valor, and you, Jerry, will be awarded the Medal of Honor. What you three have done for this country and the world has not gone unrecognized. I have been talking to Larry Walsh, head of NASA Weather, and he has informed me that he would like to retire and has recommended you, Jerry, to take his place as head of NASA Weather. Larry has further requested that he will stay on as a consultant to you for as long as you may need him. If you agree to take on this job at the Cape, it has already been authorized to give you a home right down the street from Larry in his neighborhood.

"I know things have been moving very fast and you have been offered over a dozen different jobs working for Los Angeles news stations. If we carry any weight at all, it is our recommendation and our desire that you head up NASA Weather. So many wonderful things have been happening in the last few days, I'm sure a lot of this is overwhelming. There will be representatives from more than sixty different countries tomorrow at the ceremony to honor you three. Most of the countries that will be honoring you tomorrow have already deposited into trust funds for each one of you significant amounts of money as their appreciation for saving the world. It is my pleasure to tell all three of you that you are multi-millionaires.

"I know that your names will be in history books for all of time. I am sure that the whole world owes you for your great sacrifices and heroism in the sight of such an awesome threat. I know most people who have been put in your position feel that they have done nothing out of the ordinary to deserve such honor, but it is my opinion, and the opinion of most countries of the world, that you truly are genuine heroes. And we want to show our appreciation and our indebtedness to you all."

CHAPTER 13

After the ticker tape parade, the ceremonies, and all the joyous time spent in the past six months, Tom, Jerry, Lydia, and her father started living regular life once again at the Cape.

Tom went back to Long Beach to head up the West Coast Weather Watch Search and Rescue for NASA weather. Tom and Jerry stayed in contact with each other, regularly working together and building for a better future.

Larry Walsh finally had a lot of time to do the things he always wanted to do while helping Jerry with all the things at NASA Weather that Jerry needed help with. He also stayed close to his daughter, Lydia, and saw her happiness grow daily.

Jerry's children had become jet setters, spending half of their time in Los Angeles and half of their time with their dad at the Cape.

As for Jerry and Lydia, they couldn't be happier. They got married and live in a very nice home at the Cape. Lydia has just found out that she will be a mommy in eight months and has decided to become a housewife and mother. In her words, "A wife to the most wonderful, handsome and daring man on the planet."

As for Jerry, I'll let him tell you in his own words.

"I am the most blessed man on the planet. Just when I thought my life was over, I found that it wasn't. I give all praise to God for my second chance at life, that when there was nothing left for that old man I had become, the Lord turned it all around, even through the course of a terrifying experience. All the years that my passion had been weather, storms, storm systems, and weather patterns, I now understand that reporting the news and the weather had just been the training for what I had to face. The mistakes that I made in my job and with my first marriage were to be the training for all the ways not to live. You see, I have spent my life hiding, as if it was in a bottle or hiding behind a camera or hiding from my responsibilities to my ex-wife and my children.

"The Lord gave me a new beginning and forced me to use all that I had known in life and showed me how to trust in him and all that he had taught me as a child. You see, the Lord gave me the tools to work with from the beginning. I just didn't use the tools properly, nor did I seem to care about anybody but myself. Now that the Lord has given me a new life, he has given me everything back that I had thought I had lost. My ex-wife and I are friends. My wife and I have two children who love and respect me, and we're working on a third, and we spend much more time together than we ever did before. My life at NASA Weather is beyond compare. Lydia and I are blessed, and the happiness and joy that we feel together can only be given by the grace of God. God truly answers prayers. I am truly today a grateful man."